"Fluently translated from the Spanish, this absorbing novel with a Holdenesque narrator delivers a raw and arresting new voice in literature."

—*BOOKLIST* (starred review)

"Dazed with grief, a young woman pours her heart out to a beloved friend who committed suicide, in a stream of consciousness that scatters the page with the ashes of home, popular songs, horrific news items, movie plots, pets, vermin, and exes. In this pitch-perfect performance of a chilly autumn homecoming in Patagonia, Jennifer Croft conjures a millennial voice that is raw and utterly real." —ESTHER ALLEN, translator of *Zama*

"*August* is enviable in its unpretentiousness, feminism, and intelligence. I texted photos of almost every page to my friends. I wanted to live inside of *August*, and am now Romina Paula's biggest fan."

—CHLOE CALDWELL, author of *I'll Tell You in Person*

"In Romina Paula's *August*, the narrator addresses us as 'you,' the missing person, in an urgent, generous, often funny voice rife with confidences, reminiscent of an adolescent sharing important, whispered truths for the first time. This novel breathes with feverish life."

—MAXINE SWANN, author of *Flower Children*

"This hyperlocal and/yet global tale of the lonely pressures of womanhood and loyalty bristles against sentimentality while insisting how much we must turn to language to realize emotion. *August*'s confessions are rinsed in the waters of the intellect and give a large purchase on readers' imaginations: a book of deft fury and defter beauty."

—JOAN NAVIYUK KANE, author of *Milk Black Carbon*

AUGUST
ROMINA PAULA

*Translated from the Spanish
by Jennifer Croft*

FEMINIST
PRESS
AT THE CITY UNIVERSITY
OF NEW YORK
NEW YORK CITY

Published in 2017 by the Feminist Press
at the City University of New York
The Graduate Center
365 Fifth Avenue, Suite 5406
New York, NY 10016

feministpress.org

First Feminist Press edition 2017

 This book was made possible thanks to a grant from New
York State Council on the Arts with the support of Gov-
ernor Andrew Cuomo and the New York State Legislature.

This book is supported in part by an award from the National
Endowment for the Arts.

First printing April 2017

Cover and text design by Suki Boynton

Library of Congress Cataloging-in-Publication Data
Names: Paula, Romina, 1979- author. | Croft, Jennifer (Translator),
translator.
Title: August / Romina Paula ; translated by Jennifer Croft.
Other titles: Augusto. English
Description: New York : The Feminist Press at CUNY, 2017.
Identifiers: LCCN 2016046248 (print) | LCCN 2017005001 (ebook) | ISBN
9781558614307 (paperback) | ISBN 9781558614277 (ebook all)
Subjects: LCSH: Voyages and travels--Fiction. | Female friendship--Fiction.
BISAC: FICTION / Literary. | FICTION / Contemporary Women. |
FICTION /
Coming of Age. | GSAFD: Bildungsromans.
Classification: LCC PQ7798.426.A89 A913 2017 (print) | LCC PQ7798.426.
A89
(ebook) | DDC 863/.7--dc23
LC record available at https://lccn.loc.gov/2016046248

The girl returns with a rodent's face, disfigured
by not wanting anything to do with being young.

—HÉCTOR VIEL TEMPERLEY,
Hospital Británico

AUGUST

1.

It was something about wanting to scatter your ashes; something about wanting to scatter you.

Your dad told me that yesterday when I met up with him, that thing about the five years. I mean, I already knew that, you know. I just hadn't been thinking about the legal limit being up. We were drinking white wine, I don't know why, maybe we were both in a kind of stupor. I don't like white wine, it's the worst. We went to one of those places with fluorescent lighting and yellow walls, just because, because it was there, and because it was heated. We weren't getting anything to eat, we didn't eat, it was too early for dinner and too late for coffee and snacks. And anyway we'd already committed to the wine. The white wine. So as you can imagine it hit me pretty hard. The wine, the ashes, the combo. Your dad tells me that now it's legal to exhume the body, your body, that you can finally be exhumed and, I mean, dealt with. How since the waiting period on an exhumation has expired they can now remove you from that anonymous grave and actually deal with you, deal with your body. He says they want to take you out of there to scatter you, elsewhere, sounds like they want to scatter you from somewhere else or bury you. I don't know, that part wasn't super clear to me, I don't think they know exactly, either, what to do. But that he wanted to tell me, in person this way, and invite me down to your place, that I shouldn't worry about the cost of the trip, if I couldn't cover it, that they would like for me to be there and that money was no object, that it's important for me to be there. And that he wanted to involve me in it, too, in the decision, and what did I think.

Five years, I mean, fuck, I can't believe it's been five years. I obviously of course have something to say about all this, or not even something but a ton of things, a ton of years without discussing it, or merely just in passing with the same couple of people, of course I have plenty to say.

I try to talk, seek a position I can take, knocking back my wine for courage, a big gulp of the Chablis to your pops and all his kindness, him looking out the window, saying he has all the time in the world, and he's relaxed, and right then is when I start to feel it, hard, an irrepressible despair, and I don't want to cry in front of your father, just when he's got it together, I'd hate to go and cry on him. I don't know if it's the white wine that makes it happen or what, I mean my shaking, because I've been able to say your name for a while now without losing my composure, even been able to talk about what happened, about what happened to you, to say *after the death of* rather than *after the thing with,* which, as we know, tends to lead to confusion. Or which in any case does not name it, that, the utter vacuum. You know? Even now I can say, name, write it all down without getting too worked up about it, but just right then, I don't know, your poor dad. Maybe it was the element of surprise of it too, because of course I was happy I was going to meet up with him, I wasn't really prepared for anything sad, or excessively sad, so it kind of took me by surprise. And the wine, I never drink white wine. So he tells me the thing about cremation and asks me what I think, that he wants to know my thoughts on it, and, you know, I make an effort, I try and pull myself together, keep control of my mouth and my jaw. I say, I'm not sure how, that I agree, that whatever they decide is fine by me, because ultimately all these rituals that have to do with death are more for the people left behind than they are for the deceased. And that if that's what they thought would be best, if cemeteries had no particular meaning for them, as a place to go and visit, as a point of reference, that they should do it, that it was fine by me and that it actually seemed like a good way to get closure, considering how it had been five years. I said something in that vein, adamantly, I think, I guess because of the wine, I spoke with conviction because I wanted so badly for my sadness not to show. I just hope I didn't overdo it. We did a toast, and I was trying to go back over *Six Feet Under* in my head, back over the way they were able to naturalize it, death as an everyday thing, kind of to try and get myself to chill, calm down. But it was hard, for some reason I couldn't quite make it to that ordinariness the Fishers were able to have. After that we talked about other stuff, and I did hold it together until it was time to go. When your dad gave me a hug my knees started shaking and almost gave out on me, like they did that day. I was overwhelmed, and he noticed; it was a lot for him, as well.

First, and I don't know in what order, I'm watering a yard—this is in Esquel, it's the yard from our house in Esquel, or a blend of my dad's house with your place in the country. I water the trees around the edges of the property. I remember what order those went in, which came after which, and the sensation of traveling from one shadow to the next, and where there was grass growing and where there wasn't. The eucalyptus, the oak, the pine, the pine tree with its fruit that comes in little flowers, pine flowers, brown, wooden, like wooden flowers; the space for the gate, with no trees, the vegetable patch, the succinct patch of raspberries, which doesn't produce much, that tree with the symmetrical branches, parallel to the ground, easy to climb, and its sticky orange and yellow fruit—are those its flowers?— and then the fir tree, like the pine but blue, which couldn't be climbed and therefore made less of an impression, had less personality, to those of us who sized up trees in terms of practicality. Everything is very dry, and it's hard for me to control the hose, because it's big, wide, and the water pressure is high. Was it yellow?

Then I'm in college, at school, and somebody taps the tip of one of my teeth, one of my front teeth, a little piece that seemed like it was loose, and that's how they all fall apart, the whole front part of my mouth shatters into little pieces like my teeth are made of glass. The leftover shards remain in my mouth, spiky and sharp, like rodent teeth but broken. Surprise and pain.

2.

I hear mouse sounds all the time. Which translates into: I would like to move, get out of here. Ramiro doesn't feel that way. Ramiro thinks it's stupid. He maintains that any city will be full of mice, let's just thank our lucky stars it's not a rat and that we can resolve it by not keeping things in the pantry anymore. Yet meanwhile, every time I come across another package of something that you can tell has been nibbled on by the tiny teeth of vermin, I feel like throwing up. And like leaving, moving. Ramiro says every time there's a problem, no matter how small, instead of thinking how I might be able to fix it, I just want to run away. That may be. But I can't think of any real solution here. And besides, it's not the only one. The only problem, I mean. Besides, what he calls running away is probably just my instinct for self-preservation. So for me ultimately the mouse invasion confirms the state of total disrepair we have the house in now, how disconnected we are (me at least) from where we live in order for another thing to take up residence, another being. And if it's not that, then how do you explain why it never happened before? I can hardly think it's a coincidence. Or maybe it is—or maybe what it is is an accumulation of coincidences that in turn form a sort of mouse grid. I have a dream about rodent teeth, and then one night, standing at the corner where our place is, I look up and see a mouse running along the wires like they're pathways, with that determination, that certainty. A few days later I come upon another one, another mouse in another neighborhood. Frozen. Tense. Close to a cable. I put two and two together, understand it got electrocuted and fell, splat, onto the sidewalk. And then, from the bus, I see rats—these are rats, these ones are enormous—and I see them circulate, emerge from an abandoned building, and head for a mound of trash bags, absconding with something, absconding with things, food, coming and going, real fast, lightning fast, one with a piece of bread. I can see them multiply before my very eyes, there are more of them each second, forcing me to think about the rodent, about our rodent. Is there just one of them or are there more of them? Maybe it's a family. Making themselves at home, I mean turning our pantry into their home. I'm resigned, I want to leave the mouse the house, I don't want to kill it, I don't want to poison it; if it winds up dying in the kitchen I'll still want to leave. It's so revolting, it's done now, the havoc has been wreaked: the mouse is there, we've seen each other now, we've looked each other in the eyes, now I can neither kill it nor have it killed, even less so live with it. So I surrender the kitchen. I'm think-ing, now, about—was it in *Bleu* or *Rouge* where the girl comes across a mouse, or maybe even a mother mouse with baby mice in the pantry or the laundry room (I can't remember exactly what it was), and it completely freaks her out? At the time, as I was watching it, I didn't get why it was such a big deal, why she would make such a big deal out of a few little mice. Then I think she borrows a neighbor's cat and goes and shuts it in the room with the mice for it to do its thing, and I remember that she really freaked out when she did that, I guess because she had kind of made this mental association between the mother mouse and herself. That was definite-ly *Bleu*. Although if it were *Rouge* it would be the same, I mean identifying with the mouse, so many tragic women, girls who suffer, all of them tragic.

I don't want to live here anymore. Ramiro says we should do that, just bring a cat in. That if I feel sorry for the mouse like an idiot and refuse to kill it or poi-son it, then I should at least let nature do its thing, let the cat do its job, and we won't even see it, we won't even know, and anyway, says Ramiro, it prob-ably won't even happen because the mouse probably won't even come back if it smells cat. That could be. Ramiro reminded me of how when somebody broke into our house, back in Esquel, it was basically the same thing in the sense that back then, too, I kept on saying we should move. I had forgotten, but that's true, that was a long time ago. Indeed, the sense of intrusion was horrible for me, not because of the things themselves, I don't even remember what they took, but indeed, it did take me a long time to get over it, the fact that they came into our house while we were sleeping, while we were there, all three of us, because there were still just three of us when that happened, Dad hadn't gotten married again yet. I not only couldn't sleep the night after the robbery but also for many, many nights afterwards. It's not that I wasn't sleeping, I guess, so much as that I kept waking up at the same time really early every morning. I would go to the VCR in the living room that had the time on it in big green letters, they hadn't taken that, I guess they'd heard some noise or something that had stopped them before they got to it or whatever, in any case they hadn't taken it. Anyway, I kept waking up at the same time, like by some internal alarm, always in a kind of panic, and I would get up and go down the hall and into the living room, where we had the TV and the VCR. I would look to see if the green light that the VCR gave off was still the same, if the trajectory of the light of the numbers was the same as before, if I could recognize it or if there was anything obstructing it. If it was okay, then that was a sign that we were going to be okay, at least for that night. If not, if there was something obstructing the light, or if it just wasn't there, then we'd been hit again. It was like that night after night, while my dad and my brother just went on sleeping, unaware that I was roving around, that there was someone ranging around the house, that there was a person watching over them and looking out for them while they were sleeping. I don't remember exactly how long that lasted. Obviously I didn't mention my nocturnal meanderings, I never told them anything, but I did insist for a while that we move. For me at that time that home had reached the end of its cycle: that was where my mom had run away from, that was where she hadn't wanted to live with us anymore (not there or anywhere else, now I know that, but back then I didn't quite yet have that clarity), and as if that wasn't enough we'd started to be vulnerable to the outside, too, to external threats. And that was more than enough for me to deem it cursed. Deem the duplex. The cursed duplex. But Dad's reasoning was always a lot more levelheaded and concrete than mine: Where the hell did I think we ought to move to? Conclusive. And he reversed the theory on me: our house was actually now safer than any other, than all the other homes we could ever possibly reside in, because the chances we'd get broken into again were one in a thousand, one in a million. I don't know, this argument didn't really work on me, but at the time I had no option other than to go along with it. And then, I don't know when, but at some point I stopped waking up at three in the morning, and then that was it: I was over it. Dad still lives there. My reasons for having to leave were probably the same as his reasons for staying. At the same time I think he really believed in his probabilities argument. And now Ramiro reminds me about that, about that other time that I insisted that we leave, and how then I just got over it, how then it sort of simply fizzled out. It's true, and besides, there's not much I can do without him being on board. I can't live alone. And I can't live with Manuel. So I'll probably take your parents up on their invitation. A few days down south might do me good. Meanwhile the cat can do its thing. I personally prefer not to be around.

3.

Before leaving town the bus makes a stop in Liniers. The seat I chose isn't bad, all things considered. It has a number of pros: it's upstairs, more or less in the middle. There's no one next to me. The only little con, which I do detect immediately, is that right exactly where my part of the window is there's a divider—I mean, the window, the glass, is bisected smack-dab where my face is. This is bad because the view will not be optimal, although I still think I did okay, in terms of safety it's a good thing because it's a divider that could absorb a blow, you know, if it ever came to that. It's a divider that isn't glass at least. So I reconcile myself to that metal/rubber strip standing between me and the landscape.

Getting out of the city itself is hell, it takes an hour to get from the station in Retiro to the neighborhood of Liniers. *Emilia from Retiro to Liniers*, that could be the name of another movie. In that hour, Clemente, the attendant charged with making our bus ride more comfortable, busies himself with welcoming us and explaining that they will be serving a hot dinner, followed by coffee with a whiskey option after for the movie they will show, then breakfast on our approach to Bariloche. Clemente is very excited about his job and about his microphone, he's very excited to be able to tell us everything he tells us and to be able to do it over a microphone. Clemente darts between the rows of seats and insists we not deposit solid waste into the toilet. He repeats this. He says: We repeat, no solid waste. The prohibition alone upsets my stomach. The seat is wide and there's no one sitting next to me, the bus isn't that full, they have wine to go with dinner and whiskey for later, but all of this that bodes so well in the beginning quickly turns into nightmare: Clemente feels obliged to entertain his passengers nonstop. Like we can't just look out the window. When he's not talking on his microphone, he's walking around passing out things, taking up things, offering us refills, asking if we're too warm, if we're cold, if the AC's okay. I try to look out the window so that he doesn't talk to me, and he ends up suggesting I shut the curtains because of the rocks. Rocks? There's nothing outside but prairie, not even any little towns. There's not even a landscape to look at anymore. So then I try to get into the movie, which has been on for ages already and has this man with all these arm muscles trying to play nanny to a group of extremely blond children who are having none of it. He has bottles in his belt like grenades. It doesn't work. I'm not into it and I can't sleep. Clemente comes and goes.

For god's sake, Clemente, enough already. There are some people who are actually snoring now. I realize that the trip I had pictured and hoped for is not going to happen now. That that thing about looking out the window and letting go and permitting my mind to wander freely is no longer possible. I'm trapped inside a moving box that smells like armpit and has Clemente drifting around all over everywhere. And I'm tired, but I'm not sleepy.

I disobey Clemente and crack the curtains. You can't see much, but I have to distract myself from the bodybuilding nanny. I want to be able to get some distance from Buenos Aires, let Buenos Aires go, in order to be able to understand my situation there as it actually is. I think about Manuel's face by the side of the bus at the station, think about his faded jeans, his tennis shoes, his curls, remember how he looked at me, waited until right as we were leaving with his hands in his pockets, the candy—the little umbrella-shaped candy and the chocolates—that he slipped into my pocket when we hugged that final time. I feel like I already miss him, which happens with those relationships where you see the other person so much they become a necessary outgrowth, which is the thing about them that's not good. It throws me off or at least just throws me for a loop to have his body be in fact so far away from mine. I've gotten out of the habit now, that's what it is, I'm out of the habit. I'm out of the habit of being by myself. Now, on this bus, I begin to be aware of something like Manuel withdrawal. And yet, is he the person

I choose, would I choose him now, from scratch? Could I in fact now choose not to choose him? Did I choose him, did I choose all this at some stage? How did it even start? I can barely even remember how it started. Through Ramiro, I guess. That's right, at some party. After a number of evenings, of course, and afternoons of drinking yerba mate, too. From me taking no notice of him to me not paying much attention to him to me being obsessed with this other guy from school and not seeing Manolo as anything other than one of my brother's friends. To finding out all of a sudden because my brother tells me, reluctantly, almost in spite of himself, that this guy, this Manolo, really likes me, that this curly headed kid just really likes me and has been asking after me. And then I'm caught off guard: I hadn't noticed that he liked me at all, I had never thought of it, not at all, not ever, never for a moment had I thought of him as a possible prospect. To getting drunk later at some party and ending up kissing him, after some concert, in Banfield or in Lanús, to me throwing up, and him taking care of me and wanting to keep kissing me even after I had thrown up, and then coming back on a train to Constitución one Sunday morning, my face resting on his jacket or his scarf or in between his jacket and his scarf. From not having thought of it ever before to sleeping with him and then being inseparable from him from that moment forward. Two years now, since that morning, and I never once so much as reflected on it, not before, not after, not during, everything just sort of drifting along, of its own accord, and I started to grow fond of him gradually until suddenly I was very fond of everything, and we never really parted after that time we kissed up by that stage after that concert in Lanús. Or in Banfield. Where I liked that he took care of me when I threw up, that he kept kissing me after, and that he held my hand on the way to the station, with my purse slung over his shoulder, to help. I liked that he was holding my hand already, like we were together, liked him taking certain liberties I let him take because I was drunk, because I wasn't feeling well, and also because I also felt kind of good, that, too.

Clemente wakes us up in the morning, not without violence, putting on a DVD of Latin music videos. I open my eyes, and besides Patagonia I see Ricardo Montaner in white on some Greek terrace, which is very white, singing to this dark-haired girl in a flowy dress attempting to look attractive, on some beach somewhere. Ricardo sings on boats, at sunset, in interiors with terracotta vases. Clemente comes and goes, ever diligent. His hair is styled, he's put some effort into it. He sets a tray on my lap while I try to get rid of the groove the window frame left on my cheek. My forehead is moist and my hair is all squashed. My forehead is damp from the condensation on the window. Outside, the mountains. In about an hour we'll be in Bariloche. I had a strange dream, which I can't quite remember, but something, lurking. Some familiar sensation, something recovered.

When I get off the bus in Bariloche, the wind from Nahuel Huapi Lake rustles my bangs, and the icy air unstops my nose, fills it with the smell of people. I feel the cold in my teeth, open my mouth, drink it in. Breathe in a mouthful of southern air. I'm starting to feel good. Now, from here, from this station, while I wait to get my bag back, Manuel, with his pants and his curls, seems far away/removed.

4.

Monday. I'm not quite sure how to settle in/be in your house, I'm not exactly sure what to do. I try to stay in motion to regain a sense of familiarity, I make the rounds. Your cat doesn't recognize me, she keeps her distance, and if I go up to try and pet her she bites me. She sleeps with her back to me. She insists on this. I guess I deserve it for having left her behind, for having cruelly stopped coming, as though Ali'd only ever been an extension of you. I empty a couple of ashtrays; your mom told me to make myself at home, of course, and that I could do whatever I felt like, and to make myself comfortable. But obviously it's not my home, and I can't even be sure now that it was ever really yours. Your dad even lets me use the computer, just imagine how sensitive he's feeling right now in order to leave me the password on a little yellow paper, one of those with the sticky strips across the top, for reminders, with his imperative that I memorize it and destroy the evidence at once. I don't really know what to do, I appreciate his generosity and I appreciate—knowing him—the magnitude of his gesture, but for now I'd rather write by hand. It's such a big deal, that computer, that I'm afraid something might happen to it. Your dad, that maniac, put a sweatshirt on the monitor, can you imagine? One with *UCLA* written on it, absurd, it must have belonged to one of you guys, they put it over the screen so the cat wouldn't scratch it.

Today I snooped around in your stuff, but like, just because, like demelancholized, like my eyes were dry, as I was snooping, just checking things out, taking a look. I came across that drawer you keep filled with scraps of paper and things, the one that has all sorts of movie tickets and little invites and little notes, a million of my little notes, pure nonsense on them, so much nonsense written down, the reconstruction of a history of stupidity, basically, of silliness, of whatever. Plus notebooks, all begun but none completed, with just a few things written down, just a couple, in frantic handwriting. Thoughts jotted down frenetically, that's what it looked like, things written in moments of duress, fits of rage, based on the penmanship, because it was yours but different, not like yours at school, not like yours in letters, which had so many things crossed out, so many mistakes and things you changed your mind about, retracing your steps, your words. Here it was all nonstop, no going back, like you hadn't even reread it, not caring about errors. You were writing feelings or dreams, I don't know, just different things. But that wasn't it, it wasn't what you were writing that surprised me, I actually even re-membered some of those situations, I guess you must have told me some of those dreams. The weird thing is the tone, the way. That's the weird thing. That's not the way you talked. It's also not the way you wrote, not when you were writing to someone, to me, for example. Lines brimming over with anger and despair, hatred, almost, very severe, with your-self, with everything, but above all with yourself. So hard on yourself, my goodness, what force of per-sonality. And yet, it was actually a happy discovery for me, I mean, it was good. I mean, I should say that at first it made me feel insanely strange and deep-ly sad to think I hadn't really known you, but of course that isn't true, of course that would also be ridiculous, because let us just agree I did know you, because, I mean, if not me, who? And then that end-ed up being what I liked about it, that there would still be things about you that I had not yet had the chance to find out. I liked that, the fact that you would not have shown me everything, or revealed it all to me, that there would still have been some things that you had kept to yourself. Look at what a little mystery you turned out to be.

Yesterday I had another dream about the peo-ple from *Six Feet Under*, but just Nate, David, and Ruth. Ruth reminds me a lot of your mom, and I guess now my unconscious must have conflated them, because in my dream Ruth was Ruth but she was also your mom and the guys were kind of like your cousins. At any rate we were at your place in the country and the sprinklers were on, and I was getting wet, I was kind of showering under one of them in a dress with this pattern of green leaves, kind of like the outfits that Fräulein Maria made for the Von Trapps out of their old curtains. I was rinsing off under the sprinkler, and I was really happy. Nate and David were around and Ruth/your mom was too, but she was inside the house, I knew she was in there, and I felt a deep affection for all involved. Then someone, it might have been you, was asking me if I had a crush on anyone, and Nate was taken, because Brenda was there in my dream as well, your mom was talking about her and saying that she had hooked up with who knows how many other dudes, and I think it was you who was asking me if I had a little crush on David. We both knew he was gay, but it didn't matter, I liked him so much that I did kind of have a crush on him, and Nate too. So stupid, the characters, because it wasn't even the actors in this case, just these characters who end up somehow being a part of your life, you know? But in any case the Fishers reminded me of your family from the moment I first saw them, nothing I can do about that.

5.

I haven't stopped sleeping since I got here. I can't, I just can't stop sleeping. It's a little bit embarrassing, because of your parents, who knows what they'll think, that I'm depressed, maybe, I don't know. Maybe not. Your mom leaves me a breakfast plate on the table with a little note whenever she goes off to work. She's incredible, your mom. And I have the most bizarre dreams because I just don't stop, I cross over from dreams into something else, I get into something else, into this very bizarre state. I mean, it's your bed, it's your house, your room, it's all super strange, very weird. Even though it doesn't really look like it did before. It's been sort of neutralized, you know? I feel like, between the fact that your sister kind of lived in here for a while and the fact that it seems like it's being used as a guest room now, it's just become sort of transient. I always liked it that your parents kept your room going, like that they kept it up to date, so that way it's neither yours nor not yours, I don't know exactly how to explain it: it's yours, but neutralized, taken down a notch.

And yet you're still there in certain things. Certain pictures are still there, the ones you cut out of magazines, the Berni you got from a magazine, or Pettoruti maybe? I don't remember, and it doesn't say, the one you cut out of the magazine, but it's still there, tacked up on the bookshelf. Bulgo's picture's still there, too, under the plastic part of the desk, and next to it there's a piece of Johnny Depp's face that you can tell somebody tried to remove, but Johnny held on to the plastic, really gave it his all, and there he is, he's still there, young and beautiful. There are a few more things. Mostly in drawers. But I already told you that. They didn't give away all your stuff. Your mom kept quite a bit of clothing, some of it she wears; I took a thing or two too, back at the time, the blue pullover with the little balls, which I slept in until really recently, it's pretty disgusting at this point, but I still couldn't toss it, even if it means nothing now, I mean, the pullover. It's weird to see your clothes, really odd, to see them here again, more or less intact, and just the very fact they still exist.

I talked to Ramiro, and it sounds like the mouse hasn't left yet, but he has taken a couple of concrete steps. He bought a mousetrap (ugh, an inquisition), and he put a piece of cheese in it; he said the mouse hasn't tried it yet but that now the whole kitchen smells like cheese. Meanwhile he put out poison for the mouse to eat, and he mixed it with who-knows-what-type of seeds for the mouse to nibble on, but apparently he was told that the poisoning takes whole entire days to happen, because the mouse takes such small bites it takes it a long time to die. This is horrifying. My humble household has quickly been transformed into a site of terror, institutionalized death, and everything, I don't know, I find it disgusting just to think about. But Rama sounds pretty stoked about it. Like he's gotten reacquainted with his bloodlust, his former vocation of roach catcher, that masculine thing/virility.

Today my plan is to walk around a little, get out, see if I run into anybody, by chance, I mean, although I kind of hope they don't recognize me, like I won't be going around ringing people's doorbells; there's very few folks I would actually like to see. After that I'm meeting your parents for dinner. Julián, for example, Juli's somebody, one of the people I would (most) like and not like to see. Ever since I got here, since we started coming up on the valley, like even back on the bus, on that morning, as soon as I woke up and there started to be mountains I suddenly had the strongest sense of Julián, as though it had simply been anesthetized, put on ice or something, or in salt, that sense, all this time; I woke up and my nose had fogged up the freezing window, my face was cold and squashed, I scattered the condensation on the glass with the sleeve of my jacket, I saw the first light of morning over the peaks, not yet reaching the highway, and I felt—god—that memory in my body, in the view, everything, sense memory, sensations lodged there, memory mocking plans, mocking decisions.

And now that I think about it, those strange dreams I had last night also included Julián. I don't quite remember what he was or anything, but I exited those dreams with still some sense of him. What I don't get though is if that means I'd like to run into him or just the opposite. I know I'd like to hear, but just hear, what he's been up to, but anything I might do, any movement I might make, could run the risk of being misinterpreted. I'm afraid of calling him and having his wife answer, I don't know if he's married, I don't even know if he's still in Spain or if he's back, and if he's back I don't know if he came here or stayed in Buenos Aires, I doubt it, that I highly doubt, but I don't know, I just have no idea. I don't want to ask your mom, I don't know why, exactly, I guess I'm slightly humiliated by the thought of her thinking I'm still into him or whatever, I don't know. Maybe it's not even that, maybe there are just certain answers I don't feel like hearing, who knows. I hate that these things are like this, so tough, ex-boyfriends. The strange thing is going overnight from sharing everything with someone to no longer knowing anything about what they're doing, the person you shared everything with and knew everything about, every day, everything that happened every day, and then, suddenly, from one moment to the next, nothing, and not even the option of giving them a call, or maybe you can call them anyway but then everything gets awkward, even the most basic things become uncomfortable. Losing all claims on the other person, losing them, completely, just like that, like it's nothing. I hate that, that artificial death, that rehearsal for death: forcing yourself to accept this idea that that person's disappearing, has disappeared, is gone from your life, and you no longer have any reason to expect to hear anything else about them ever. It's absurd and overwhelming. If they're still alive and still around, or even elsewhere, you want to know how they are, what they're up to, I don't know, something. Right? Isn't that the logical response? I'll see, I might end up going by his place this afternoon, by his parents' place, to see what the situation is, I could end up ringing the bell, potentially find out something.

6.

You know how cats always position themselves in the most attractive spots? Exactly where you'd go if you were similarly sized. Right now your cat is curled up in the sink. She's in the sun that way, and she's arranged herself over a blanket your mom left there to wash. Meaning it smells like people too. It couldn't be more ideal. Who was it that said that man living in the city is a mammal living like an insect? I don't know. I do know that being here you're overcome by sleepiness, no two ways about it, and I am now a viable contender with your cat in terms of hours of sleep. I sleep a lot, as though being awake no longer held any attraction for me.

Yesterday I finally ended up going for a walk, around the neighborhood and a little bit beyond. At first I tried to kind of avoid all the potential problem areas, my route determined by all those spots I preferred to not pass by. I went around the city center, crossed the boulevard, walked along the outside of the bus station, and then I started going up, went from asphalt to dirt road without really realizing it because it starts with just the asphalt getting quietly underneath the dirt and the gravel, and then suddenly walking, taking steps, has a soundtrack, raises dust. I went up a little ways towards the lake, but the sun was intense and I started sweating, but I also didn't want to take off any of my clothing because the air was cold, and my T-shirt was already damp, so I came back, back downhill, and started towards the highway, towards Trevelin, wanting to see a little of the countryside. Everything is so exactly the same . . . If it weren't for the sneakers I'm wearing that I definitely purchased this year, I might doubt my age, doubt my historical moment, the point on the line of my life where I am currently positioned—I'd doubt the line. But there can be no doubt about it, there ought not to be, these sneakers are new, new soles, they're red, I picked them out, recently, Manuel went with me, it took me three hours to decide, he and the salesperson conspired against me, mocking my indecisiveness, while meanwhile I was dealing with another type of issue, I knew I wanted these ones, the red ones, but they were expensive and I felt guilty, but at the same time there was no point in spending money on others because these were the ones, and then I had an argument with Manuel because he'd been on the side of the idiot sales guy, Manuel being like, come on, it wasn't that big of a deal, how I'm too sensitive. Thus these shoes became my shoes, shoes of discord; therefore it is me in the year two thousand something, there can be no question. But outside of me it's all so chillingly exactly like itself. It's so cold here, I'd kind of forgotten how that felt, my lips are already chapped, the corners cracked, and I can barely open my mouth, such a dry cold, and so cold. I sit by the highway for a while, in some grass, in the shade but with my legs in the sun, and if I smoked I would definitely smoke a cigarette. I fish around in my pockets for a piece of candy, but they contain nothing, nothing edible. I swallow and miss how candy tastes and how cigarettes taste, in my imagination, anyway. It smells dry here, weed-like, mountain-like, hay-like, southern, a smell barely discernible due to how dry it is, so dry it nearly impedes the possibility, the constitution, of a smell, of a fragrance. This absence of moisture, this suction, this cold, could truly drive you insane, truly induce it. Moisture, moistness, makes things work, brings things together, permits them contact. With prolonged exposure to this cold and this dryness, to this dry cold, connections sooner or later stop working and then I want to see you with your centrals nervous, nerves frayed, and this desert in the back of your forehead.

I find myself on Juli's block. His parents' place. Everything is exactly the same: the dirt road, the same houses, everything the same. They put in some bars here and there, but apart from that it's identical, even the same dogs, and I'm inundated/

overwhelmed by sadness . . . I don't know if it's a bad sadness or a good sadness, it definitely makes me cry, but I couldn't really say if that's out of relief or despair, the kind you need to avoid and leave behind or just a good sadness, I don't know what it is. In any case I am a little glad to be here, weird, like this sense of my own self in my gut, of ownness, of recognition, of belonging. Something. And while I'm trying to deal with all of that the bars part, I'm already at the corner, and automatically I dart behind the hawthorn that's just in front of me. I don't think about it, if I had I wouldn't have opted to look so ridiculous, but fear leads me directly to stupidity, to acting stupid. So now that I'm here and everything I do will look suspicious, I pay homage to the Benny Hill–ness of the situation and peek out from where I'm hiding. But what I see when I do so is vastly less amusing than Benny and a blond losing their clothes behind a bush: I see his mother leaving the house with a kid in her arms. Jesus. I know it, I knew it, it's Julián's, it's Julián's, I know it, I know it, no one needs to tell me for me to know. Jesus, fuck, and meanwhile I am hiding in a plant. So pathetic, the story of my life: other people start families while I cower behind a bush. What's worse, I spy. I want to run away, but that would probably draw a lot more attention, so I don't. Susi sets up her grandkid in a stroller, kind of tucks him in, hesitates, and then finally heads off in the other direction. I stay for a second in my hiding place, more out of bewilderment than anything else. I look back at the house,

no sign of life inside though, now, and for a split
second I consider ringing the doorbell. Just to get it
over with. Say, hey, how's it going, I wanted to meet
your new family. Hey, what's up, so you're a dad now.
But no, I couldn't handle it, or I wouldn't want to. So
I'm off, I head off, leave the foliage behind me, leave.

7.

Education as formative. Hours and days and years in institutions; lots of long hours per day and not much aside from that. Education. Inhibition. How they work. Together. One at the root of the other. Being afraid, fearing. And, at the same time, wanting to steal your friend's boyfriend. Wanting to tempt him with a fruit—from which tree? On the playground—of which school? One of those with the fruits like cotton that comes in a double shell that closes over itself. The silk floss tree? Is that silk floss fruit? Or what is it? Is it the fruit of the green silk floss's pink flower and spikes? From one of those two-story schools with the hundred-percent-cement play area, perfect for knees. And fear, after. Fear of the teacher, above all, of authority. Fear of them kicking you out? Of them calling you out? Pulling you aside? Getting set apart? Maybe most of all that they will call you out on it. A past of insolence, an initial becoming insolent. I'll do what I want to do, I'll do what I want to do, I'll do what I want to do. A first act of insolence or challenge to authority or lack of recognition of hierarchies, punishments with switches. By force: force of words, of order. Threats. Of what? With what? When they say: what you're doing isn't right. Not only that, but also: it's wrong. When who knows what—in a human being—is actually wrong.

Like in that article about the big serial killers, vicious, greedy murderers. One of the examples was Ted Bundy, a very smiley person, suntanned, such a go-getter; another was that old couple who killed children in England. What were their names? Point being, in the article there were these specialists who said how there's a certain grade of wrongness that will not fit into any psychological framework, that is of some other order, unclassifiable: pure wrong. Unadulterated wrongdoing. It was kind of like they were freaking out about it a little bit, these psychologists; they didn't even want to get into religion or morality, which would lead nowhere. They talked about psychopaths, some who'd end up killing, others not, and of course some of those serial killers are not even psychopaths. And there was a kind of scale they'd developed that went from one to twenty-one in order of severity to calibrate the degree of cruelty shown by the killer to the victims. After that I wondered how psychology positions— where, how—death itself, a person's own death, I mean. One's own death. What place it holds in the brain, in the mind. A person dying for him- or herself, an intransitive. The reflex of a person's death, the reflexive act of dying, dying as reflex. Dying is therefore reflexive. I guess that's something.

8.

I mean. The ABCs of my psychology, my building blocks. Yesterday I saw Juli's mom with a kid, with a baby, and today I wake up overwhelmed by him, because of him, because of dreaming him, exhaustively and at length. Dreaming seeing him, dreaming him talking, me still going through that same old awful thing of not being able and not wanting to simply let him go, and at the same time not wanting to stay with him. Or not being able to. I don't know. The with-or-without-you thing, that whole thing, with or without you. Like Fanny, like Depardieu. That pit in your stomach, in your heart, that hole where nothing ever, nothing you can do is or ever will be enough. Ever. That sense of reduction, of absence. That's what I felt, that pit, I felt it in my dream, having Juli there in front of me, and at the same time I was happy, I mean, a specific sense of happiness, so towards him, seeing him there, being face-to-face with him and knowing that I wasn't going to shatter into a thousand pieces, at least not yet. That sensation too—that of my heart in my throat just from wanting to know, basically, if he's okay, what he's been up to. So in my dream we were talking, and he was telling me that he had kids and a wife or I don't know if he was saying that, but the feeling was that he was with someone, and that there was something that wasn't possible anymore for the two of us, that was it, impossibility, and, nonetheless, the undeniability of that which does remain, of what we do still feel, that chemistry, that charge, that need. It's like I could ingest, devour him in those moments, so he would stay inside me forever. Or have him kill me, I also think that, I think that that could happen, and it's almost like I want it to happen, like I'm expecting it to happen, for him to kill me. If I close my eyes or rest my head on my arms on the table, and he smoothes my hair, I think or I feel that in that moment he could crush my head in one fell swoop, kick me directly in the head and kill me, but I don't open my eyes, I just stay there with my eyes shut, not feeling fear, only resignation, surrendering to that, surrendering to him, to his capacity to crush me. The death drive, I guess, and I guess it always felt like that with him, that death drive. Like being at the midpoint between wanting to avoid and needing to go ahead. Knowing, hearing that it would be good/would be better to get out of it, and nonetheless not being able to, not really, not being able to escape, and going going going on and on and on, as though magnetized, by something. Maybe the kid's not his, maybe Susi was watching some other kid, why would it have to be her grandchild? Yesterday I didn't have the guts to ask your parents any questions over dinner, I kept feeling so shocked about that baby that I didn't want to talk about it at all, I'm sure it's his, that he's the father, and I need to kind of get used to the idea before it gets confirmed for me, I need to be able to handle the confirmation in a stoic manner, when it's given. Right now I'm a wreck, I'm not sure why it's killing me this way, obviously it was always there within the realm of the possible. I mean: he isn't and wasn't a part of my life anymore, even if he was before, and he's free to do whatever he wants, and I always wanted him to do well, to be happy, or maybe not happy because maybe that's too much to ask, but I did want him to get to some sort of stability, I guess, at least an emotional one. But now it's hell for me that he has that, it makes me angry or sad that I couldn't give it to him, and worse, still, that he's been able to find it with someone else. Fundamentally, I can't tolerate the idea that he's had children with another person, another girl, another woman. The idea that there could be little hims in the world, and that they would have nothing to do with me, is painful, I don't know why, or I don't know why it's so bad, I guess I hadn't ever really imagined it, I'd always assumed he'd be kind of lost in the world, trying to reconstruct his life, and now it turns out that he didn't waste any time at all, didn't waste a single second, and obviously he wouldn't have been on his own for this whole time, with his charisma, which you've got to give him. The son of a bitch is enchanting. Ali watches me, eyes wide, in that cat's pose that's somewhere in between complete surprise and watching like a hawk and beholding the face of a corpse. I find it funny when she looks at me like that: I hold her gaze, try to replicate her bewildered face, and for a while we just stare at each other. I wonder if she's trying to convey something to me that I can't quite understand, or whether she sees something in my face that I don't know about. It's such a bummer, this stuff with Julián. It really bums me out. He always really bummed me out. The same thing that attracts me to him bums me out about him, that's it, really. What I find attractive depresses me, or I'm depressed by what I find attractive, I don't know, I don't know what order everything happens in.

Anyway, so dinner with your parents was great, albeit with me performing acrobatics the entire time in order to avoid or not broach certain topics. Basically they asked about my life in Buenos Aires, if I liked it, if I'd adapted, who I was hanging out with there, they noted how few people had made it in the city, that most of them had come on home (danger: Julián), they asked if I was happy with my job, and here I glossed over some stuff and only told them all the good parts, filtering out my fears, for their sake, emphasizing my flexible schedule and that I did with my time as I wished, that that really was great, and then they asked me about school, or no, I think they asked me about that first and with that I really laid it on thick, extolling all the many virtues, all the many benefits of institutionalized learning, citing more what I recalled of my hopes for college when

I was about to go as opposed to what I found in fact upon arrival/ended up with. That yeah, I liked it, that yeah, it was taking me a while to graduate, that I still don't have a board to lay stuff out at home but that I do have a big table, that when I have to I work at a classmate's house, and that yes, I have met a ton of really cool people, and that there are all kinds of people, there really are, most of them from Buenos Aires, but from other places too, that there are just a lot of people period, so you get a little bit of everything, although I guess not everything everything, it's an expensive major, the materials are all really expensive, yeah, really outrageous, and that my dad has to keep sending me an allowance for all the materials I need for my different classes, that, I mean, I got a scholarship but that my dad pays rent as well, which is a huge relief because if we had to pay rent we couldn't go to school at all, definitely not. That yeah, that Ramiro is still in college too, but he's kind of setting his own pace, taking it easier because he's really into music right now, that he met some guys at school, I mean, he met one of them there and then through him the others, his group of friends, most of them from Buenos Aires or from the suburbs, all musicians, mostly rock, yeah, they have a band. Yeah, it's great, Rami's really into it and plays all day some days; he just bought a used keyboard from one of these guys, so now he's doing both guitar and keyboard, and he's beginning to compose. No, it doesn't bother me at all, I actually really like it, I like the music they make, and I like having music and people around, that's the main thing, is that I really like having people around. No, it doesn't really bother me when I'm trying to study, that I either shut the door or go to some classmate's house or some café, but in general it doesn't bother me anyway, it actually helps me focus, I'd say it relaxes me. That in fact my boyfriend is the drummer for their band, so it could hardly bother me. Yes, exactly, Manuel, oh, yes, I'm very happy, that recently things have been getting serious between us. No, he's from Mendoza, but he's been living in Buenos Aires for forever. He's just a little bit older, two years older than Ramiro. So that's what they do, they have the band, they've been playing for quite a while, just that Rami joined them relatively recently because they had a fight with their guitarist, who was also their singer, so it was Rami and this other guy who sings who joined the band at the same time. He sings really well, it did the band a world of good to make that change, this guy really has an incredible voice, totally unique, and he also gets so enthusiastic about the band, about the group itself, in terms of the people too, which is really important. Reducido, that's the name of the band: Reducido. Yeah, they play quite a bit, on the south side mostly, I mean of Buenos Aires, and in little nearby towns as well, they play quite a bit in small towns, they get quite a few gigs. Yeah, they usually do play with other bands, they're still not appearing on their own yet, or I mean, very infrequently, but it doesn't really make sense for them yet, they're not that likely to draw enough of a crowd to pay to rent the space and move all their stuff around, I mean, one of the guys has a truck, so that transports all the equipment, but even so, the idea is to make some money, even if it's just to maintain all their instruments and such. And for food and what have you. Yes, I'm super happy, Manuel and I are going very strong, oh, yeah, he's very laid back, yes, yes, I really care about him (danger: Julián), he cares about me too, we care a lot about each other. No, yeah, he also works in a store that sells instruments, on Talcahuano, yeah, right smack in the middle of the city, that there are a lot of them there, yeah, that he gets a little bored, but it's not that bad considering. And it's actually not under the table or anything. And besides it's only temporary: he wants to start teaching music classes in schools, he likes kids. So I mean I definitely can't complain, and your mother says how it's so great that things are going so great, and I say, no, absolutely, I definitely can't complain, and cheers, I say, and they say cheers.

We walk home, because we'd gone to the place on Rivadavia, which, of course, still has that old Nicolás as their main waiter, who told me how I'd changed, kid, while meanwhile staring at my chest, which made me fairly uncomfortable, but anyway we came back on foot, and you can't possibly imagine how cold it was, and your mom laced her arm through mine, and your dad was holding on to her, and that was how we walked on back to your place, all of us drunk, almost a family.

I still can't figure out if I am happy or sad. All I know is that I'm here. I'm here, that's the one thing I am sure of.

9.

Ali and I have developed a similar technique. It's strange. When I wake up she's the first thing I see, usually she's still asleep. She sleeps until she feels me moving, and then her eyes part slightly, usually she can't be bothered to do much more than that, so she sizes me up for a second or so, sees that everything is in its place and as it should be, that my waking up this time is not significantly different from any of the other times, and unless she yawns or stretches or shifts a little she'll just stay perfectly still. Then I stretch out or writhe around a little in your bed, toss and turn and roll over and over, and then I simply watch her, being peaceful. I wonder which of us is guarding which at night.

Today Vanina came to see me, and it was super weird. Not that she would come, of course, because apparently she had heard I was around, and then she asked your mom, and it's not like your mom could have lied to her, and plus she had no reason to do so. So she came, and we drank mate. It wasn't that bad, in the end, once I'd overcome my initial panic or whatever it was. I mean at first I was utterly inhibited, I don't know, she was happy, purely and sincerely happy just to see me. I mean, in reality, of course, things aren't actually that complicated. Or at least they aren't for everyone. She seemed good too. I don't know why I say *too*, I don't know if I'm doing good, I don't know, you'd have to ask her, I guess, how it was I came across. For the moment I prefer not knowing. Anyway, the point is that she's still there, I mean, here, but that she's happy, happy with her decision to stay, to not go to college, to not go off somewhere to go to college, like most of us. She said that at first it was really tough. And besides, at the time she was going out with Mario, and Mario was going to La Plata, and she started to go for it, she thought about going with him, but in the end she didn't, she ultimately decided to stay because actually, when she was being totally honest with herself—her words—she couldn't think of a single good reason to go, since she loved Esquel, she always had. But that it's only been in the past two or three years that she started to be really good again, that at first she used to get depressed because she wound up kind of lonely, feeling like she'd ended up here by herself, and she was working, but she was kind of depressed. She was working as a waitress. But then apparently she started seeing the owner of this bar, it's this new place, on Rivadavia, orange, kind of dimly lit, that has a pool table, anyway, but so she started seeing Omar. That at first they were seeing each other in secret because Omar was married, but then apparently they fell in love, and then Omar left his wife, and Vanina and he moved in together, and now she's like thrilled living and working with him. That at first people had been judgmental, but then in reality nobody actually even liked Omar's ex-wife, who went back to Madryn, because she was from there, so really the majority had been on her side, like they'd mostly been supportive, but regardless she had not been too concerned because she knew the gossip would die down after some time passed and everybody'd just relax. And that's exactly how it happened, now they're really happy with the bar, which is doing really well, and on weekends people even come from far away, which is good for them, and she says how they bought a little car and a tiny plot of land on the outskirts of Esquel, and the idea is to start building a house on it, slowly but surely. That they don't want kids, yet, that it's just been very recent that they've been able to chill and be alone together, after all that ruckus over his divorce, and that they'd like to spend some more time just like that, but that, yeah, she did figure she would start a family with him, that she saw him as the father of her children, and that actually, oh, and by the way, did I know about Julián? Here I make sure that my face doesn't change. Julián, I say, what do you mean, I have no idea what you're talking about, know what? And she gets this little twinkle in her eyes, that twinkle of getting to be the one to break the gruesome news to me. Oh, so,

Julián's got kids now, two of them, or, well, one with another on the way. My blood starts running cold, then the predictable/old pit in my stomach. But I keep feigning control. So weird, right? Julián as a dad? Who would have thought, says Vanina. Meanwhile I, bigger liar than ever before, say, what do you mean, I don't think it's weird at all, he'd probably be a great father, I don't see why not, and then she unintentionally drives the dagger in deeper, works it in slow: well, you know, yeah, actually that was the surprising part about it, was that it was incredible seeing Julián with the little one, he takes him everywhere he goes, and that it's kind of beautiful to see. I feel like I would like to die, or at least like I would like to kill this messenger. And yet the juiciest part is still to come, and I know that Vanina isn't going to tell me, or that she isn't going to say it of her own accord, she'll wait until I ask her, let me want to know, let me demonstrate I want or that I need to know, so as not to gratuitously wound me, as though the damage weren't done. Even though, based on the information I've provided her, about my boyfriend in Buenos Aires, plus the time that's passed, plus my performance that I'm giving now, the amount that all this hurts me shouldn't show. She doesn't, cannot realize. She assumes, I think, that I love my life of a free agent in the city, believes that it's a life I wouldn't trade for anything, which I guess is what I have been trying to convey to her since her arrival, what I've led her to believe. And really anyone—even me on a good day—could easily confirm this, that I wouldn't trade my simple, pleasant life in Buenos Aires. It's just that right at this precise instant I'm not so sure. What if all the decisions I have made were bad ones, and I should have stayed with Julián? In which case those children, those kids, would be mine instead. Jesus. Kids with someone else. Which means he's inextricably connected to another woman. Which brings us back to . . . Who'd he get married to? Oh, no, he didn't, or, well, that now he had, that now he was indeed legally wedded, but that that was after, after the son was born. León. León, he's apparently named, what a nice name, what a discreet name. Very Julián, he must have chosen it. Bound for all time to another person, another woman, deeply revolting, Jesus. No, the girl is younger, you wouldn't know her, she's from Trevelin, Welsh family, they had been going out but not for long, really, that the girl was just eighteen, that she'd been eighteen when she'd gotten pregnant, and that they'd decided they would keep it. She had wanted it although she'd just completed high school. Mariela, her name is Mariela. Now she's twenty-one. And so yeah, León was born, and when he was a year and a half or so, they got married. That no, Vanina hadn't gone to the wedding, that they'd invited very few people because they didn't have any money, and because her family wasn't too thrilled about the marriage, about Julián, or the fact that he'd knocked up their daughter prior to proposing. So they hadn't made a big deal out of it. She'd stood at the altar with the baby in her arms.

Ah. Pain, the most profound/the lowest kind of pain. He'd just stayed with her? Since when is he capable of that level of love? Well, but I mean, it's his kid, clearly nothing's going to get in the way of that. His kid. So anyway, so here they were, he'd brought her down to live here, at his parents' place, and for now she isn't working, Susi's helping her with León and with her pregnancy, and Julián is working with his dad, mostly with the truck, deliveries, traveling a lot.

Good, traveling. That might mean that not everything is so perfect in the end, it means he spends a lot of time away from his family, that makes me happy, that is a relief, Jesus, this should make me feel vulnerable, and yet it doesn't, it doesn't because I feel at the same time like the story of my life is all dissolving. And Manuel? How is it that he could just evaporate like this from my mind and my present and my desires, my desires above all? In two years it never even crossed my mind, not once, to have his children, and I assumed this was a stance on my part, a lifestyle that I wanted. And now I come here and after a couple of days I'm already feeling like I'd give up everything to be the mother of those children, the woman in Julián's life, his wife, the one. The workings of desire are curious. The workings of stupidity, as well. That yeah, that Mariela's nice, the wife, or well, she doesn't know her that well, but that she seems nice, that in fact she doesn't talk much, that she seems very shy or whatever, Vanina's heard she comes from a very strict family, tough father or something like that, so she's not that used to talking. That she barely goes out, that she's always with the kid, and besides, she has complicated pregnancies, ending up on bed rest, so it's also not like she has been around that much, because between the months of pregnancy and then recovery she's been in bed almost nonstop, ever since she got here, she's essentially just been lying down at home, and it's not like Vanina knew her from before, so all in all she just can't really say. Yeah, she doesn't really seem that healthy, it's kind of overwhelming when you look at her because she's twenty-one but looks more like a little girl, like León's older sister, so it's kind of intense to see her pregnant, all emaciated but with that belly, and here I wonder how Vanina's seen her if she's been on bed rest, but it doesn't matter, maybe Vanina just contents herself with picturing the girl so skinny and big bellied, it is enough to overwhelm, I also feel a little overwhelmed imagining her belly swollen and her face that of a child's, the light hair of a little girl, with freckles, I guess I picture her as Sarah Polley, but at thirteen. Like Sarah Polley when Sarah Polley was thirteen. Less healthy. Poor thing. I note I already feel affection for her, and I have the weirdest urge, on the one hand, to go and sit with her and tell her stories or read to her while she's on bed rest, while on the other hand I want to smother her with a pillow or give her a bunch of tranquilizers or sleeping pills so she gives me back the world, so it gets given back to me, the world and everything that has to do with it.

So my chat with Vanina, the chat itself, wasn't that bad, but it got blurred in the background behind all the images that popped into my head, populating your parents'/your whole living room. We hugged, I promised I'd go by the bar one night, she left. I locked the door, I went to the bathroom because I didn't know what to do, I took off my clothes, every last piece of clothing, and I got into the shower, like a robot, like an idiot, as though anesthetized, I don't even know. I'm pretty sure I didn't cry, I couldn't cry, I think I wanted to but couldn't. I was in there for a while, under a stream of water I kept very hot. Ali lay there, calm, curled up in the clothes on the floor. I looked at her. She looked back, her eyes wide open. I threw up.

10.

Yesterday this house was host to a big barbecue. How could you not want to be here for that? The ashes from the mosquito coil make the same shape on the big tiles on the floor, a spiral of ashes around a little sheet of metal that just looks silly now, purposeless. The ashes are still there, they haven't scattered, they're still exactly where they fell. Your cat does twists and licks her lips on the patio floor. So captivating. I stop and cover her with kisses. She sheds, and my mouth gets hair all over it. Tricolor hair. Cat hair. Now she cleans herself, licking between the pads of her paws, her claws, her little claws, licking her nose.

In the end the ceremony's going to be on Sunday. Yesterday your sister came, which was what did it. I was pretty out of it, I couldn't really connect, but I still shared my opinion. They couldn't decide. Your parents, especially your mom, had this idea of just putting the ashes in the ground by the poplar in the back, why make such a fuss, that she liked the idea that the ashes would remain there, at the house where you'd lived all your life. Your dad didn't say much, I think he was fine with it, or in any case he couldn't come up with anything better. Your sister had already said she wasn't too super excited about any of it, just in general, that to her it was just dredging things up for no reason, that she had already made this known, that they already knew, that so whatever they wanted to do was fine. That they could just let her know when on Sunday, and where, and that was that. That she'd come for the barbecue and just to see her parents, and to say hi to me, too, of course. And that that was it. Meanwhile I—who knows why—waxed poetic. It surprised me they weren't more decisive, or, at least, more imaginative when it actually came to the ceremony. Especially considering they had suggested it. I said that I liked the idea of scattering your ashes from the bridge, into the river, that it might sound cliché or whatever and that I knew it wasn't a place that could be all that much associated with you, per se, especially compared with your house, but that I didn't know, that I knew you did like going there, to the river, that ultimately it was the thought of your ashes falling freely and scattering out over the valley, of them flying, that was the good part about it; that putting them in the back behind your house was after all a way to bury them, and that maybe it would be good to take the ceremony, the concept of the ceremony, to more of an idea of freedom. I also said, on a roll now, that I remembered this movie I'd seen, which wasn't about this or anything, but that this somehow reminded me, or for whatever reason I just associated the image. A movie where at the end, in the last scene, the girl throws herself off a kind of bridge too, in the mountains of Mongolia or wherever, the movie was Chinese, the girl was Chinese, and she was committing suicide, but it wasn't a suicide, or anyway it wasn't sad because she was flying, she stayed suspended between the clouds that were there, floating in the air, and it was sad and poetic and beautiful. I didn't say all of that, I decided to omit the suicide and poetry. Your sister, who had her mouth full, said that that was fine with her but that we'd need to go right around noon because when the sun's not hitting the bridge directly it's simply way too cold. Practical. Your mom got a little bit emotional, you could tell it was a little harder for her to think about this getting rid of—because it is that, too—your ashes. Your dad thought it was a nice idea. So then, ultimately, so did your mom.

11.

Today I dreamed that we were going on our high-school graduation trip and that in my hand luggage, in the outer pocket of my carry-on, there were two rats: one was real and the other fake. I just left them there. Maybe it was because I talked to Ramiro last night. Apparently the mouse isn't gone yet, and there's just no way that Mauro's cat can be convinced to hunt it. It won't even get close to the kitchen. I found this funny, Mr. Tough Cat. A cat fully domesticated and well-fed expected all of a sudden to have instincts it's in no way capable of having honed. Meanwhile apparently it's really made itself at home at our house, it spends the whole day sleeping, apparently it particularly likes the floor where my room is, the little steps and the chair from under the table. Ramiro talked about the cat like it was a person, which I really found funny, apparently they've bonded. He asked me about Dad. I told him, I told him about going over there for tea, about our kind of tricky hangout at home that afternoon, in Dad's home, in our home, ex-home—whatever, there. Carmen was fortunately not there, I mean not for any real reason, I like her perfectly fine, it's just easier to relax if it's just Dad, even though relaxing, what is commonly known as relaxing, is not exactly what we did, either, in the end. The kids were there, our teenage half brothers. Delightful but demanding. Perpetually in motion. It's incredible, you can tell Dad's fully back now. And Lorenzo, such a teenager, can't catch a break from those hormones, is my impression, you just can't even imagine what an attitude he has. Not with me, obviously, in fact I felt like he was trying to form some sort of alliance with me while I was there, but with Dad he will not quit, it's crazy. Facundo, no, Facu is huge, but he's still like a kid, he must be five nine now, but he's very childish, which of course is an explosive combo. He messes around all the damn time, sits on top of you and totally squashes you, he's like a mammoth wanting attention all the time. He does a pretty good job of getting it, he's very funny, plus he and Lorenzo have this routine going, of sorts. Lorenzo acts like he's Facundo's father and calls him snot-nosed all the time, Facu goes nuts, they spend the day kicking each other's asses, it's funny to watch, although I can't even begin to describe to you how tiring it gets. I went in for tea and came out exhausted. I still have my adolescent-brother quota taken care of, I haven't gone back to see them since that afternoon. I promised to tell Dad when I'd be leaving, he wanted to invite me over for a barbecue or something, so I guess I'll see them then. Dad seemed good. Pretty relaxed. Or maybe just the contrast with his children/ quasi-grandchildren. Clearly having the family keeps him sedated, as it were. And Carmen, she's also very hyperactive. Apparently they now have other couple friends, something like a social life, like they go out to eat and stuff, make these social plans, and Dad wears these little shirts, and corduroy, very cool, a kind of more robust Woody Allen, Carmen's clearly the one in charge of outfits. And he has fully given in to it. As though it were another life—in fact it is, it's another life. It's fine, I'm happy for him, it's good. After tea and the interlude with the brothers we sat for a while in his study with the door closed, my ex-bedroom (so much ex right now, so much), and there we were able to have more of a real conversation. He told me about his new life, he laughed a little, at that, his new role, saying that sometimes when he's tired he locks himself in his study and everybody knows not to bother him. That he has a really good relationship with the boys, that he's enjoyed, that he's enjoying fatherhood again a lot, the fact of living with these kids. That sometimes he regrets not being able to be more fully present when it was us, that he had so much going on back then, that what happened with Cora was really very hard on him, not just because of us, but because of him as well. I tried to avoid that subject, but on the other hand my brother and I are the only ones he can talk about it with, so I let him talk, let him go back to that, and I tried to make him understand, again, that we truly hadn't ever wanted for anything, that

I have the fondest memories of him as a father, that I have no resentments towards him, but it's no use, he feels he has a sort of debt to us, and there's no way to convince him that he doesn't. But he was fine, it's not like he got too worked up about it or anything. He told me he'd started writing again, that he'd been doing that and that he was happy with it, but he wasn't discussing it with anyone because they mocked him, that Carmen didn't get it, that she thought it was just some stupid thing that old men did, that they started calling him Neruda when they first got wind of it, just stuff like that, so now he only writes from within the confines of his study, he says, without showing it to anyone, but he's happy, he says for now he doesn't feel the need for readers. I asked him to show me something, told him I'd like to read something he's written, see what he's been working on, and he told me not yet, that he's still revising, that maybe later on, that yeah, that he'd show me something, but he insisted—it was conditional upon this—I was not to give him any feedback, not to tell him what I thought. That he was embarrassed, and that in any case, once it was ready, once it was done, he didn't have any intentions of altering it anyway, that it was all just what it was, that that would just be that. What about you? he said, he wanted to know what I'd been working on, if I was writing, and I said, very little, that I didn't really have much time for writing, that between school and the boyfriend I had very little time left for myself. Though then that struck me as funny, the thing about time for myself, since all those things, boyfriend/school/work, were mine, were me, and it's strange I would refer to them as things/activities taking me away—or at the very least distracting me—from myself. I stopped talking. I kept thinking about that. Time for myself, what could I have meant by that, what could I have been referring to, exactly, when I said time for myself?

The Counting Crows CD showed up. I mean, I guess it must have been there the whole time, but I just found it. It must have fallen behind something or whatever, because I'd already looked through your CD collection and hadn't spotted it, and then suddenly, out of the blue, there it just was. Your mom must have been tidying up in here the other day, and then what do you know but I'm looking for something to listen to, and there I spot it, spot its yellow spine, just as though it always had been sitting there. I play "Round Here." I can't believe it, from all the way back then. I remember that woman from the video, walking with a suitcase, in a city at first and then on this esplanade, I remember that the best, that esplanade like a desert. I don't remember exactly if that was where this girl was, I think so, she had this dress on, and then at some point she was falling someplace. Falling into water? I don't fully remember, I do know the overall sense of it was of total desolation. She was devastated, she was a lunatic, you had to love her for it. Was there a guy there too? I don't know why I feel like I remember a guy wearing a suit, I think it was a brown suit, but honestly I really couldn't say if he was there or not, wearing a suit, in any case the song takes me back to this desolate sensation of a man in a brown suit in a vacant lot or on a salt flat, and he was so inadequate, uncomfortable, and out of place. I listened to it a few times in a row, Ali watching me cry like a moron, poor thing, until finally she came and sat on my lap. Then it got worse. I pet her very vehemently; at the third drop that plopped onto her back she decided to move on to a safer place. Her indifference did me good, it sort of snapped me out of my melancholy. You would have snapped at me if you had been here, told me that the Counting Crows are lame and that you'd stopped listening to them in nineteen ninety-five. Which is fine/fair. All I can say to that is that it's easy to refuse to be sad when you're only planning on living for such a short amount of time.

12.

Families that eat some of their members. Every so often there's a case like that: some family that eats one of its members. This time it's in Britain. In some suburb. So like a functional family with everything set up/all settled, perhaps a tad overnumerous: mother, father, and eleven children. One of them, the twenty-one-year-old, is married to a twenty-year-old, Rachel, who had just given birth to their second child. Their last name was Huchon. At some point she vanishes, from the world, from her family. The Huchons say she ran away, that she just left their household. But that's not true, they keep her locked up there. They torture her. They beat her with a baseball bat, they burn her with cigarettes, and who knows how many other things we'll never know because although her body will divulge some information, it is scant, and she herself can't talk now. This happens in March. They find her, or more precisely, they find a body, some time later on the grounds of an abbey. At first not only can they not tell that it's Rachel but also they can't even tell that it was female, such was the degree of decomposition. Oh, and it was wrapped up in a carpet. And then the series of cover-ups one would expect given it's a family and how blood runs thicker. This slows down the investigation, which nonetheless arrives at its conclusion, verdicts being reached. The most severely punished are to be the parents, her parents-in-law. Her husband, too, some of her brothers-in-law, and, a little lighter, some of the other wives, too, for covering up or slowing down the investigation, I can't remember all the details. But think of all the things Rachel won't ever be able to tell us. Of the teeny-tiny amount her decomposed body was able to tell and everything else it kept quiet. Why had the family chosen her, her and her alone, as their martyr, after she'd given them two children. Had they all been equally sadistic? Had her husband protected her or been the overseer of her torments? Could she have run away or gotten help before the final absolute imprisonment? Was she, in fact, absolutely imprisoned? Or just unable to escape? What in her made her succumb to that family and not be able to save herself? The story of those who carry these things out, who perform these acts, who take things all that way. Eat another person to keep going. And so as not to have to eat the meat of their own flesh and blood, they go for the next best thing. Poor Rachel, rotting away while still alive, poor Rachel. Like hamsters, like hamsters eating their own offspring, that same thing, eating your own flesh, feeding off oneself, being/becoming one's own sustenance.

13.

Ceremony, barbecue, so it went. First the ceremony, then the meal.

On the bridge it was cold like you wouldn't believe. I didn't mind that, though, that factor, the wind. Because it kept everything short and to the point, making the longer thing the meal. Which was nice. Your dad didn't grill this time, we went out to a grill so that nobody would have to work, that's what they said, so that your mom wouldn't have to wash any dishes. So we went to the one on the boulevard, which wasn't that good, apparently they have a new owner now, but that didn't really matter. Your sister was there, although as soon as she was finished— she didn't eat much—she went ahead and left; and my dad came too, but by himself. I didn't know he was going to be there, apparently your mom had invited him, a surprise of sorts, I'm not quite sure for whom. Me, I guess. I got sort of slammed from all sides today, although none of it could take me down. I didn't shed a single tear, even if I would have liked to. It did affect me, I won't deny that, especially there on the bridge, since the launch thing was my doing, scattering you into a free fall, and I had that image in my head of that Chinese girl falling in among the clouds, I couldn't help but feel things, but I guess I felt so much I didn't cry. I guess it would have been cheesy to cry, or like, redundant. Or like I suggest the ceremony and then collapse, around your parents—it wouldn't have looked right. It was more of an internal commotion, being moved inside, as though something, your ashes, was plunging down while falling, as though falling inside me, as well, as though I had fallen backwards into my own depths, or something, with no gravity. That persisted awhile, that sensation, that of falling inside myself and continuing to fall, while the thing with the ashes couldn't have taken more than a couple of seconds, that's what I mean, your vanishing act, which just took a couple of seconds to complete. One two three and they were gone, and you couldn't distinguish a single particle of anything, of that, that matter, you. No one said anything, we didn't move during the descent or the evaporation or I guess I don't know what to call it, during the thing, and then we stayed a little longer just like that, the wind was awful, sharp, it sliced into your neck, but I was wearing a hood. Until your sister said we had to go, that she was freezing to death, and we got into the car, the four of us and your grandma, who didn't say anything at any point. I don't think she fully understood what all was going on. Can't blame her. And from there we went to the restaurant. My dad was dressed up, with a few days' worth of facial hair, but very well-groomed. Clothes ironed and painstakingly coordinated, a senior ladies' man. The Carmen factor. He barely drank any wine and talked a lot with your parents, about various things, other things. I didn't have much to say, I really didn't, and nobody asked me much of anything either. I was such a kid in that context, with all those grown-ups. Which allowed me to be quiet, to not have an opinion about anything awhile, I probably could have even fallen asleep with my head on the table or sprawled out over some chairs and nobody would have even batted an eyelash. As a matter of fact I was on the verge of doing so, that's how much I was feeling the kid thing. Then we took your grandma to her nursing home, and she kept on wanting to know where she was going, poor thing, that was a difficult part of the day, with her wanting to know if we were going back to her house or where, and your dad saying, no, Mom, don't you remember, you're living in a home now, with Flavia, the nurse, who's eagerly expecting you, remember the nurse you like so much, who makes you laugh, and your grandmother saying nothing, very absorbed, not understanding what she was being told, sticking her hand in her purse to fish around for the keys to the house she no longer has. I stayed silent on the drive back too, all of us were silent, we dropped my dad at his house, and I lay down to sleep awhile, still fully dressed, here in your bed, I couldn't take any more, I didn't want to think, I really just didn't want to keep thinking. I had very turbulent dreams, the kind you have during a nap sometimes. I was awakened by nightfall.

When I got up I felt an overwhelming anguish, unbearable, so bad I couldn't see straight. Sunday nights are sufficiently intolerable in themselves, even when you sense them coming, as night approaches; but having the bad luck to wake up in the middle of a Sunday evening that's already in full swing, already going on, with night just there— there's nothing that compares with that. I stayed seated on the edge of the bed for a few seconds or minutes, not comprehending what time it was. I saw that the clock said seven thirty, but I didn't know if it was morning or night, I couldn't figure out when I'd fallen asleep in the end. The light from outside didn't really help me either, the semidarkness could have corresponded to the beginning of the day just as much as to its end. What settled it was Ali: Ali wasn't there, and then she came in, just then, coming right into the middle of my mental fog and rubbing up against me, very awake, very alert. In the mornings she wakes up with me, so I figured it must be night. So it was still—ugh—the same day. Still the twenty-eighth of August. I went to the bathroom, looked at myself in the mirror, verified that I was overheated and that I had a big crease from the blanket running down my left cheek. My hair was matted and sticking straight up. I tried to flatten it with a little water, brushed my teeth, put my jacket on, and went out to Vanina's bar.

My life is not what one would term heroic.

14.

Disgusting, he tells me. That as early as the afternoon he'd smelled this dog smell coming from the
kitchen, this wet-dog smell, but that he'd been doing
something and for some bizarre reason he hadn't
wanted to look into it. But it turns out dog smells
don't just disappear. And it also wasn't just an issue of humidity, of humidity in the room. So later,
at night, it offends again. He's washing the dishes,
and now the stench becomes unbearable, out of
the question that it's in his head. So he works up
the necessary courage and gets going on it finally.
He opens up the little doors to look under the sink;
the smell gets stronger. It reeks, there's no getting
around that. He sees the rag we use to wipe the floor
off, which we had left there to plug a leak. He lifts it
up. First grim finding: under the cloth there's a tiny
cemetery plot of mouse poop. Clearly the mouse
taking advantage of the warmth and darkness of
the rag, like it's a burrow. There's something that's
around here, then. So: he starts to take containers
and platters and what have you out from under the

sink, and lo and behold, grim finding number two: the rim of one of the serving dishes—it's a blue one, made of glass, I know exactly which—offers up this sticky mess comprised essentially of hair and something similar to skin. Belonging to a mouse. A hodgepodge of hair stuck to the glass with something that looked a little bit like fishing bait. My stomach turns. But there's no going back now, the dog smell has completely taken over. Now is the time to face the music. So: the entire lower part of the cabinet is clear (if we prefer not to think about the poop, of course, and let's just say we do prefer that), and the coast seems to be clear, at least to the naked eye. He takes the broom and sweeps under the base or whatever, a place unreachable by the eye aforementioned, and that's when he feels something. It reaches him through the plastic bristles, the wooden handle, and from there to his hands, the sense of a mass, the contact of the broom with something that isn't dust or dirt, something with a weight, that budges. He pushes/sweeps his find up and out from under the sink, all the way out to where he can see it, and there it is, in this order: first a tail, then a disintegrated body (he describes this disintegration in some detail), and finally a disgusting, disgusting little mouse head. I'm the one who says disgusting here, it's just I can imagine it. Ramiro, for his part, and as repulsive as he also found it, did seem happy to have bested the mouse in their little battle, to have regained his jurisdiction over his kitchen, our kitchen, to have conquered once again the rodent's space.

The state of the creature according to its execution-
er was (I'm sorry to be so exhaustive, but I needed
to know, needed to know what fate had met that being I'd shared my living quarters with for this in-
determinate amount of time): ruptured. Apparently
the poison, that toxic fuchsia fluid, so/too reminiscent of little anise candies, had caused an implosion
in the small stomach of the animal, and detonated
its organism from outside in. Apparently it wasn't
quite a rat, but nor did it have the skimpiness of a
vesper mouse: it was exactly a mouse, somewhere
between brown and green, according to Ramiro; a
standard mouse, I add, and Ramiro says yes, trium-
phant. Disgusting. Now I learn, because your mother tells me, that apparently there are other poisons
less aggressive to the beholder and that—instead
of rupturing the animal—they dry it out, literally,
from the inside, leaving it stiff, as though desiccated.
So, even if it takes you a while to find it, it doesn't
rot on you, and you won't find out about it based on
smell. This mouse, our mouse, was generous and let
itself be found in a very early phase of its decomposition process. Fortunately I was far away from that
death, from the grim finale of that inhabitant of
our apartment. Meanwhile Corso, the cat, has fully
settled in at this point. It goes without saying that
it refused until the very end to get its paws dirty,
not to mention its claws, its nose, choosing to keep
its distance, the greatest distance possible from the
little interloper. And yet Corso has his own theme
song now, recounting his comings and goings (the

chorus of which goes, *Corso, Corso, / come up onto my torso. / Come up and let your hair down. / Come on and then you get down. / And don't you bite me, / don't you bite me. / Please will you let me simply play guitar, / Corso, Corso. / Come up onto my torso*), an ode to the pacifist/draft-dodging cat. Such is Corso. Come up onto my torso.

15.

I go to Vani's bar, the bar she set up with her fancy new boyfriend. Your mom offered me your sister's bike when I left, but I didn't want it because I didn't want to get there quickly, that was the whole point. Besides, I was half-asleep and kind of numb and afraid of falling over. It's freezing out, of course, but it does me good, right now it does me good. I walk quickly, hiding my face clear up to my nose in the high neck of your jacket. I put my hands in the pockets and find a bus ticket. It must be yours, it's from nineteen ninety-six. A ticket from a trip to Trevelin. I get so depressed with these very short days, fourteen fucking hours of darkness, so much, so much night. With this much darkness you'd have to be Swedish or Canadian or something in order to get anything done, to want to do anything regardless, to feel like going out. All I want to do in this type of cold with this eternal nighttime is sleep or drink wine. Sleep and drink wine. But nothing else. Sleep during the day and drink wine at night. Or the other way around. That's all I'd do. That and snuggling up with someone, of course, which pairs well with both wine and being in bed. Drinking, sleep, and procreation, on with the human race.

From the corner I see a lit-up sign for a beer brand with this orangish reflection on the sidewalk. There are a couple of bikes at the door. Anybody in Esquel who's still awake—and alive—is here. I walk in, and the first thing that hits me is they're playing the Police. The Police, can you believe that? I mean, come on. I unzip your jacket, and the warmth of the bar unfreezes my face. It feels hot, I must be bright red. The Police. I glance around quickly, but I don't see him, don't detect him, and there aren't that many people after all. There is a group of kids playing pool in the back. They're younger, I'd probably know who they were if they told me their last names, they must all be younger siblings of people I know, kids I stopped seeing when they were still in elementary school and that are now adults, the boys among them even casting meaningful looks in my direction. So funny. Then there are a few couples and several drunks falling asleep on their barstools. Based on that I assume they must have been here for a while. The bar's not bad, is my impression. And there, serving as waitress and bartender, is Vanina. She's happy to see me and she comes out from behind the bar and comes up to give me a hug. I think she must be a little drunk, she must take Sundays to relax, since they don't open again until Thursday. She kind of crushes me with her hug and then says, almost shouting, as though the volume of the music required it, even though it's really not that loud, but she more or less yells and enunciates very clearly how awesome it is I came, how she's going to introduce me to her husband and that—here the level of expression in her face rises, while the volume goes down—she gesticulates, as though my hearing is impaired, he's here, she says, and I say, who, who's here. Julián, he's in the bathroom. On his own, she says. I knew it, I knew this place was bad news/did not bode well, did I not? I didn't even get to say if it was a big deal for me or not because she did it for me, investing the news with such significance that I couldn't help but get nervous, very nervous. I have to go to the bathroom, my bathroom, the women's restroom. I wrest my arm away from her and tell her I'll be back, I'll be right back, I tell her, and I torpedo towards the ladies' room. Fortunately—this had not gone unnoticed by me when I came in, and hence my strategy—the different bathrooms are at opposite ends of the bar. I don't want to be too scatological, I'll just say my nerves had done their damage, although I wouldn't want to blame it all on Julián, I was also coming up on the end of an incredibly long day, so I presume my body's rather aggressive reaction just then was provoked by the whole thing. I thought I was going to faint, I thought I wasn't going to overcome the bathroom/toilet incident. But I did, after a while, of course, and not before a worried Vanina came in to ask me if I was okay, if I needed anything, and I told her no, that everything was fine, that I guessed I had just eaten something that hadn't agreed with me, and then I added the thing about the long day, kind of to distract her, saying, too, how—on top of everything—I'd also just gotten my period. Which is true, as if the rest were not enough, I got my period, despite the fact that it was about a week too soon, and I'm normally pretty regular. Or I used to be.

Vanina says she'll bring me a pad or something, that she'll check to see what she has in the office, that she definitely has something. She comes back with one of those ones with wings and superabsorbent or ultra-absorption gel or whatever, which is a serious abomination of an innovation because it doesn't even have any cotton anymore, and that whole synthetic thing/material does nothing but collect odors. And the wings, what a terrible idea, I—whenever I have the bad luck to come across them—always cut them off. Not only did I never understand their function, but also I very quickly realized their obvious disadvantage: they lend themselves to spillage. So, when that happens, even though it's true that your underwear remains immaculate, the stuff goes straight for your pants or your legs. All I say, obviously, to Vanina is thank you. It's also not like I am in any position to reject her pad, regardless of how unfortunate I find it.

I splash some water on my face. Some girls come in, very excited, and one of them, the one that's furthest gone, shouts to the other, a girl with curly hair, neither of them's over fifteen, she says, did you see him, did you see him, and the other one says, he's so gorgeous, it's unbelievable, I just can't even handle it, I'm dying, I'm the most in love with him, bitch I liked him first, okay we can share him, okay let's share him, which is when I exit the bathroom, I leave. I assume I hardly need to add that I know who they're talking about. I play it down in my head: I couldn't care less about him. I want to not be able to care less about him. I've been going out with Manuel for two years, I think I'm in love with him, or I don't know, I don't even know if I care at this point, really, about being in love, I don't know what it means; we get along well, we have a good relationship, we're friends, we have a lot of laughs together, I don't know, it's nice. I can't let myself be affected by some random thing and let it all have been for naught. There was a reason why I left, I remind myself, there was a reason why I left back then, if Julián and I had been in love I would have stayed, wouldn't I have stayed? Just think of all the things I didn't like about him. Just think of all the things I didn't like about him: he was, well, he was selfish, temperamental, that was what it was, he was difficult and despotic, such a despot, always ended up having his way. I see him, he has his back to me, he's seated at the bar with his back to me. He has his hat on. Vanina sees me coming, she's talking to him, you can really see her with the light on her and everything. Standing beside her is a guy with a beard, must be her man, I can't even remember now what she told me his name was, what the hell was his name? She sees me coming, and I see that she says something to him, she loves it, I see that she loves being present for this moment, I see her face full of pleasure, of malicious glee. Julián turns around, he's wearing his gray hat and a very ugly T-shirt, it has like wolves on it, kind of heavy-metal style, like a Rata Blanca T-shirt. He spins around on his stool and let's me approach him. He smiles. Oh, but he is so painfully reminiscent of himself. Hey, I say to him, stretching the *ey* part out, like clinging on to the *y* in it, while I'm walking up and in the first moment of the hug. He stays there seated on his barstool, so that the height difference makes it so that he practically wraps his legs around me, I mean, of course he doesn't, he doesn't wrap his legs around me, but I can feel the inside part, the pressure of the inside of his legs, of his thighs against my hips while he hugs me, and I smell his scent, and I start to feel, to really feel, like crying. That would be the hormones.

The hey is absolutely false, and its only purpose is to slightly conceal my perplexity and to make the moment, the meeting, less important. Accompanied by a couple of slaps on the back, my will to desolemnify, to make it lighter, is negated as soon as my nose makes contact again with his scent. Fuck me. It smells so much like Julián. Immediately after the first few seconds I want to get rid of him, get out of this, get away; I want to back away, and at the first minimal movement I make I feel that he has a pretty tight hold on me, I can't go now, nor do I want to, and I relax and hug him and put my head on his shoulder, and he says, Hi, a very long hi, stretched out, sickly sweet, a hi like it's been so long, and I, instead of crying or of leaving or of at least just saying nothing, I say, Jackass, you had kids with someone else, that's not cool.

Juli laughs; "Every Breath You Take" comes on. And I just smell him. Just smell, nothing else.

I can't stand for this to be this way, I can't bear that he lucked out so that this moment, this encounter or reencounter, has gone so perfectly, that it has made him look so great, that the stars aligned and everything came together with such perfection. I can't even blame him for it. For having the bad luck that that song was the one that played right at this moment, like our moment that Sunday night, set to *Synchronicity*, when I'd burst into tears, to have my crying on his shoulder now coincide with that song in particular, given how uneven that CD is, that is fate.

That moment, of course, is completed, over and done with, doesn't exist for anything except itself, it has no past, no future. I can't believe I'm here. I could and would prefer to die right now. "Every Breath You Take" is playing, there are a lot of parts of my body making contact with his, I start to relax, leaving/resting my weight against those points of contact, transmitting everything to him, my weight, inhaling his scent, there's something of everything there, it's him, and at the same time there are a couple of new textures, something child related, he has a bit of a child-related scent about him, vomit, or something else, and a food scent, a little bit of a food scent too. Resting against my hair, on the left side of my head, there's the right side of the brim of his hat, of his gray hat. We are in silence, and he follows the rhythm of the song with his right leg, against mine, and he moves mine too. He said nothing in response to my reproach, what could he have said, he just let me cry, which was the best he could do, the only thing he could do. I keep crying, but now I just can't believe this moment, I don't understand if I'm experiencing absolute fortune or absolute misfortune. I don't know. I want it not to end, for it to never end, for it to kill me but kill me suspended there, on him, get inside his wolf shirt, his ugly wolf T-shirt, and have them tear me apart, first tear my clothes off, so that I look sexier being dead, and then me, my flesh, with their teeth, the parts of my body, I want them to devour me, rip me to shreds, to devour me completely and then sleep afterwards, full under the moon, but I don't want any hunter ever to come and open up their stomachs and put stones inside them to replace my parts because I will already be rent into a thousand pieces, because in any case no one could put me back together.

"King of Pain" comes on and the shift in the rhythm disrupts the moment. I return to the bar, I return to Esquel, and I find, much to my great disappointment, that I am whole, completely whole, exactly as I came in, at least in appearance. He looks at me, but not in my eyes, he looks at my body, he says, that jacket isn't yours, I tell him no, that in fact it's yours, and he adds that my boobs have gotten bigger. I laugh, I laugh a lot, it's true, it's true that they got bigger in the last few years, especially last year, and I think it's funny that he's noticed, not only that, but also that he has the tact to point it out to me, as he does in this moment. It goes without saying then that I'm going to wait awhile to take off your jacket, as observed as I feel, intimidated as I am. Yes, I tell him, I don't know what happened to me, the good life, he says, the good life, I say, and then, you're looking handsome, I say to him, that too, I say that too.

We have a beer. For a while I had forgotten where we were, and I'm going to keep doing it over the course of our stay in Vanina's pleasant bar, which kind of makes me feel like I'm in Texas, because of how pathetic it is, how grating, how fluorescent. Because of my jacket, because of the drunkenness, because of Manuel, because of the absence of prospects, because of how enchanting he is, because it's unreal. It makes me feel like I'm in Esquel, then, what am I saying Texas for, what am I doing, why am I trying to sound all sophisticated. Vanina introduces me to her husband, husband or boyfriend, I don't know, she calls him *my husband*, but I think they didn't actually get married. Omar comes across as pretty nice, she got herself a pearl of a fellow, a real man with a real smoker's voice. She's excited, you can tell, to be present at this moment and to be not only witness to it but also instrument of the encounter, of the reencounter. Every so often our eyes meet, she's circulating, and everything in her face suggests impishness, complicity. It makes me uncomfortable, it makes me a little uncomfortable that she is, that she assumes she is, or that she wants to establish herself as being, complicit, I mean, and that she—furthermore—assumes that it's so important to me to be sharing this moment with Julián. So that every time she smiles at me with that impish smile I look at her with no expression, neutral, conveying something like what a nice bar you have here, or how neat that I was able to come by and meet your dude/husband, something like that, something along those lines.

At first Juli and I don't talk about us. After the question I asked him and once I had calmed down and stopped crying, we started drinking beer, and he asked me about you, I mean, about your family, about your parents; he said he saw them from time to time but that he didn't really know much, that he thought they were doing fine, that they had put their lives back together, but who knows, that was just what it seemed like from the outside. And then I tell him about my impressions of these last few days, and I find myself obligated to think, I mean, to do a sort of summing up, to report my observations on how I thought your parents were doing, how they seemed, and I tell him, I tell him about the ceremony and your mom's little notes and your sister's frugality, she's kind of a bitch, Julián says, and I tell him no, that I didn't think so, that I understand her and that everybody does what they can and takes it how they can, and that Valeria is like that, a pragmatic lady, and thank god, that thank god she is, because she was able to keep going, make a life for herself, leave your house and everything and that besides all that she's a really cool chick, as harsh as she might be. So that no, that they don't seem depressed at all to me, that they're handling it well, actually, because it's also not like they don't mention you, maybe your dad mentioned you a little less, but that's his style, he's someone who talks little but that nevertheless strikes me as very communicative, with gestures, with stuff. Then Juli started asking me about my dad, and we burst out laughing talking about that new look of his, he's been seeing him around, he says that it's been ages since he's looked that good, that he really struck gold with the girl, and we talk about Carmen. She's kind of hot, the swine says, but it's true, it's true she's hot, I'm happy for my dad. Everything turned out great, didn't it? he says, and I hear the bitterness in his voice, and I realize that now I don't want to ask, that I don't want to know, that I don't want him to tell me, that I want this moment to be ours, and for there to be no freckly blonds or brats or complications with pregnancies or, especially, fatherly love. I want to talk about things I know, not attend the becoming of someone else, of the other. By this point in the encounter we are both a bit tipsy, and I'm already sweating. I still have your jacket on and decide to conquer my shyness. I take it off and hand it to Vanina, who's already standing there on the other side of the bar ready to receive it as though tonight existed only for us, a supporting character, as though we were her only guests, which we probably are, which is not good for us. Then Julián takes up the assault again. Seriously, they're bigger, girl. Yeah, well, a lot of time has passed, I say, and before I can even finish my sentence he asks if I have a boyfriend. I tell him, I tell him about Manuel, and his face is transformed, it seems to really bother him, and I can't believe it, I can't believe that he has the nerve to make a scene, to be jealous. I immediately realize that he doesn't want to know any more, and not because I've said much, in fact it doesn't really interest me either, for him to know, I'm not dying to talk to him, to argue with him, about my relationship with Manuel. He looks like a kid having a tantrum, he looks conflicted, wounded, like a child, and he cuts me off, saying, I have kids, you know? Ah, straight for the heart, a rhetorical question. But he knows, he knows that I know, but that was how everything started. Clever, on the ball, malicious, he always was, all of that. Yeah, I know, I say, refusing him my eyes, I know he's turned mean now, I understand that he feels hurt, which is why I don't get upset, his irritation doesn't upset me, but I stop looking at him, I would rather not look at him, I drink my beer and look at the glass. I get rid of the foam that's stuck to the inside of the glass, turn around, and suck on my finger. He says, let's go, I feel like going, I say okay without looking at him, assenting and licking my lip. I ask for my jacket back, Vanina says the drinks are on the house, she's pleased, I don't know if it's because we came or that we're leaving together, probably a little bit of both. We leave her a good tip, Julián puts on his sheepskin coat, and we walk out. He walks behind me with one hand on my back. I don't understand his impunity, but I endorse it, that is more than clear. I try to walk faster to get out of it, but I can't quite pull it off.

I didn't want to put on my clothes today, I wanted to wear somebody else's clothing, something else. I have a lot of daydreams, fine, and I don't know if they're good. I don't know if they're good for me, that'd be more like it. Now I'm a little sad, basically sad, and that makes me sleepy. I should write, I'm still excited and nervous, but right now I kind of feel like it would be hard. I have to get over it, I have to get over it, I have to get over it.

16.

Are you going to the Hilbs' place? Well, yeah, where the hell would I go otherwise? No, dummy, I'm asking because maybe you could be staying with your pops. No, my dad doesn't have space for me. He converted my room into his study. I'm glad, it's a good fate for a room, I'm glad that that's where he chooses to go and be alone. I'll take you, I have my truck. I haven't looked at him again. We cross the street, and Juli walks towards a truck I don't recognize, they must have traded it in, traded in the F100 for something more modern. I follow him, he opens the passenger-side door for me, we don't say anything else to each other. Inside, of course, besides being cold as fuck, it's full of snot and traces of child, and in the back seat there's a car seat scattered with crumbs, one of those seats that you buckle the child into. Oh. A real family man. The worst part is that little seat, just that little seat, which being as dirty as it is, full of life, gives me an idea of the extent of the damage. This, this seat and everything that it represents, is irreparable. I don't say anything, I move some multicolored cloth dice and a little bottle of Coke, empty, from the space I manage to sit in, I don't say anything, I hold the dice, I look at them, and in the end I put them in the rear window, alongside other things: a pacifier, a cassette tape, papers, cloths. Julián turns on the heat and the music; he starts singing Bob Marley. Midway through, he starts singing midway through. How funny, it's good to know that some things never change. Bob Marley survived it all, I see, my absence, yours too, of course, as we all did, and the adolescent mother, the difficult pregnancy, the child, the children, fatherhood. And he's still there, singing, like nothing's changed, like no time has passed, reclaiming those same things as though reclaiming everything. It soothes me that it's like that, this welcome agrees with me, it strikes me as a harbinger of good things to come, I don't know what things, but it brings something back, it brings back something good, it returns it to me. I know this song, I know by heart nearly all Bob Marley's songs, I've listened to him almost to the point of getting tired of it, although that's just a manner of speaking, because I never really got tired of it, ever. At first passively, I listened to them passively, until the only option that remained was to appropriate them, and it wasn't very difficult, I have to admit, he's easy to love. I'm a fan, I like Bob, he's a good egg, and particularly in this moment he makes everything seem a little less hostile, foreign. Juli lights a roach that he takes out of his pocket, I find it redundant, but I also think that Bob had been on before, so it's not like it's a mise en scène, particularly. In fact I like seeing how they go together, how well fatherhood and pot allow themselves to be combined, and fatherhood and reggae. He offers it to me, at first I don't want it, I think I don't want it, really I don't even reach thinking about it, it's like I had already decided the matter beforehand, I'm hardened, or I was, and now I don't even know why, I don't even remember what had offended me, so I recant, I accept the offer, I tell him that actually I do want some, and I take a nice, big hit. It's very strong. I start coughing like an idiot, I choke, Julián laughs. What the fuck is this, shithead? I say to him. Is it bad? No, I don't know, the last stuff I got is really crappy, what happened was that one of the ones at home got bugs in it, and now I don't have any. I don't have much of this left either. It's really bad. Yeah, it's fairly bad, but it seems to get you high all right. Does your wife smoke? No. Does she know you smoke? Yeah, honey, I have the plants at home. And she doesn't lose her shit? No. Your boyfriend? What? Does he smoke? Yeah, but not that much. He always has some, but he doesn't smoke much. Lately, really, he used to smoke more. You? I practically don't smoke at all anymore, I don't know, I stopped liking it. Slowly but surely. There was a time when every time I smoked I got high as a kite and it was good, it was good weed, but it gave me an irregular heartbeat or I would fall asleep or I would eat whatever, so now I hardly smoke at all. It must not be the same in Buenos Aires, he says. Well, no, I say, it's not the same. We get to the door of your house and he says, okay, okay, I say to him, and for the first time we look at each other again since the moment when I decided to be offended even though I don't remember why now. I realize then that really I was hoping or wanting him not to take me straight home, that it was just a manner of speaking, I'll drop you off, but that really we were going somewhere else, I don't know, to the river, to Trevelin, or just to drive around a little, or at least he could have parked the car for a while in front of your house, turned off the engine or something, to talk a little bit, there was so much to talk about. Wasn't there? But the fact is he neither made any move to park, nor to turn off the engine, he gives me a kiss on the cheek, very unambiguous for my tastes, and he says, take care. Take care, he says, what the fuck does that mean? Not even a see you, or it was so good to see you, or see you around, or at least a hey, I'd rather us not see each other—no, take care, he says, and in the moment it's as offensive to me as if he had said kill yourself. That's what I hear him say, kill yourself. You too, I say, and I get out of the car. No sooner do I set foot on the sidewalk than I hear him start up the truck, I don't turn around, I'm indignant. Or bothered. And besides I've become dizzy. I can't believe it, I'm confused. Did something bad happen? At what point, exactly, did that break happen, that shift?

We were fine, we were communicating, or at least that's what it seemed like, I thought so, it wasn't that we were going to fuck, I wanted us to talk, I don't know, I wanted to know how everything had happened, his life change, or okay, I don't know about the life change so much, but there was still weed left, Bob Marley, hats, and fantasy T-shirts, but fine, he was a dad, he's a dad now, and a husband, he'd have something to talk about, he must have had something. Wouldn't he? Or did he not want to anymore? He probably doesn't want to anymore, he has no desire left. This sucks, I feel so stupid, I thought we had had a connection, how ridiculous, I can't believe it. And with Vanina there, I must have made such a fool of myself, I must have looked so ridiculous, I must have looked like the spiteful ex-girlfriend, resentful, how pathetic, everybody must have realized: the kid with the family that put his life back together, or not back together, just together, given all I was was his high-school girlfriend, we were kids, how stupid, it's probably not even as significant to him as it is to me, like he just slept with me, it's very clear, I can't believe it. Right now he's probably telling his wife about the encounter, and he must have told her that I'm still in love with him, poor thing, and they must be laughing about it together, how awful, with the baby, with the baby in between them in their full-sized bed and him kissing her stomach, the stomach that holds his next child, and I'm here alone and drugged like a teenager, how fucked, how sad. I have to go to sleep, I have to sleep, I want to switch off, I must switch off.

I took my clothes off, your house was nice and warm, I wanted to forget about everything as fast as possible. I go to bed wearing my underwear and a T-shirt. I get into a fetal position, but I'm not even close to falling asleep. My ovaries hurt. So fucked up, I did it again. Or rather, he did it again. He could have, he could have had me. I can't believe it, can't believe I'm so easy. Even though I don't like his shirt, even though I'm irritated by his way, so aggressive, so constantly on the defensive, but there I am again, as though no time has passed, like an idiot, clingy. I realize, I now acknowledge that I would have liked to kiss him. I would have wanted him to kiss me in the truck and I would have wanted to try to resist him, a little, because of his wife, because of his children, and I would have wanted for him to insist, and I would cede, cede, cede to him and everything he brings up in me, everything he can do to me, and have him fuck me, like that, very awkwardly in the car, in the front or in the backseat, wherever there was more space, in front, I guess, so as not to have to cut off/interrupt the moment, I would have wanted him to fuck me like that, fast, with everything still on, the two of us with our clothes still on, and to sweat and steam up the windows of the car and to come, as I almost always did, with him. I'd jerk off if I wasn't bleeding so much.

I'm alone, I'm hungry, my ovaries hurt, and I'm

bleeding furiously and nonstop. I go to the kitchen and make a sandwich with the meat leftover from the barbecue the other day, cold, and tomatoes and mayonnaise. It's amazing. There's nothing like mayonnaise, and I feel better. My body, when it's in transition, requires fat, the more saturated the better. That's how I end the day, this long day of shock upon shock: crying and eating a sandwich, like Chihiro but sadder, because it's not even because my mom and dad were turned into pigs that I'm crying, it's for myself, because I'm nothing now/because I'm such an idiot.

17.

This one comes from an American suburb—again.
Two sisters, both that semi-ugly blond type with
eighties hairdos, very high school, with big/loose
college sweatshirts, videotaping themselves in their
living room. There's someone else, the boyfriend,
the boyfriend of one of them. At the very beginning I couldn't figure out if what I was seeing was
a reenactment or if it was really them. Later on we
find out that it really is them because everything or
almost everything that's about to happen is recorded on what I imagine is the family camera. So anyway it's Christmas, or almost Christmas, and they,
the sisters, get drunk, and a few hours later Karla,
the eldest, calls a friend of hers on the phone and
tells her something terrible has happened to her little sister, that she's passed out and choked to death
on her own vomit; that she passed out, and she died.
I see the images from Tammy's autopsy: she has
some splotches on her face, deep purple. The voice-
over says forensics says it must have been the gastric
juices, that that must have messed up her face. And
that she must have died of asphyxia because vomit

had gotten into her lungs (like Daisy, to just take the nearest example, like Daisy). Up to this point it would be an accident, a family tragedy. Shortly after this Karla and Paul, the older sister and her boyfriend, move in together, move into one of those suburban houses. There are a couple of police reports about young girls, of rape. The identikit of a young man of twenty-five, youthful blond, regular face, face from the prep-school yearbook, from the extended window where victims and victimizers resemble one another in such horrific fashion, matches the face of Paul Bernardo, Karla's boyfriend. The police ask him to do a DNA test, and they question him. Since Paul is so polite and obedient no one suspects anything of him, and they don't even look into his results. So. They get married. They go on a honeymoon to somewhere or other, someplace in the Caribbean. There are pictures and videos from the wedding, from the honeymoon. Idyllic. A few days after they get back, there's another rape in the neighborhood, but this time it's followed by a death. They find the young lady, parts of her body, carved up and buried in cement, buried in blocks of cement and scattered around/distributed in trash dumps. They can't find who did it. A little while later another girl is killed. Another young lady, blond, from a nice suburban neighborhood. And then at some point around then Karla can't take it anymore and she goes to the police. She's ready to talk. She's tired. Her husband, Paul Bernardo, beats the shit out of her, just never lays off. She says she can't handle it anymore, and she wants him to get what he deserves. And she starts confessing: that yes, she knows about the homicides and the rapes. And not only as an accomplice, but also as a participant, because she was also part of the rounds of violation and torture. That they have everything on tape. Everything. She negotiates turning over the videos in exchange for a lesser sentence. Isn't the denunciation worse? Shouldn't they augment her punishment because of that? What is the logic of commuting? Anyway, through the tapes they verify that she was indeed an active participant in the crimes. And there's more. She confesses, she has something to confess about the death of her sister. Why is she talking now? It turns out that it was actually her, Karla, who gave her sister to Paul as a Christmas gift. Paul, her boyfriend, had expressed interest in the younger sister, and Karla had decided to let him rape her as a Christmas gift, an offering for her Paul. So they gave her alcohol to stupefy her a little bit, and then they definitively put her down with some substance they had her inhale, I don't remember what it was.

They exhume Tammy's cadaver. They do the relevant tests. It's true, they find remnants of substances in her face. Paul raped her with the consent (and under the gaze?) of her sister, and that's when she threw up, choked on her vomit, and died. And here we have what may be—at least to me— the most horrifying tidbit: among the videotapes there are some from just a few weeks after Tammy's death where her sister dresses up as her, puts on her clothes, and performs oral sex on her boyfriend. He films it.

18.

I wake up, and I'm in stoppage time. Starting now I ought to be returning. To be in transit, a passenger in transit. Here I am, someone with a life in the big city, and yet for some strange reason, or for many, I don't want to return to it. To the city, to my life. I feel panicked. Now my life back in Buenos Aires makes me panic. Manuel, school, work, the apartment: I don't see what any of it's for. I can change the channel, I feel like I could do it and just leave everything, like a movie with no finale, on cable, that couldn't quite hold your attention enough to make you want to stick it out and see how it ends. The problem is that there's nothing really on the other channels either, but at least they're running different things, there's potential, there's still the possibility that something will happen. Right? I've woken up in a foul mood, I realize. Today not even your cat wanted to sleep with me. Hardly a surprise.

When I get up it's crazy late, your parents aren't there anymore. On the little note your mom left me it says: *Manuel called, call the store, when are you get-*

ting in. He wants to know when I'm getting in and
not when I'm returning, meaning he's taking it for
granted that I am in fact returning, what enviable
certainty. Return. I don't even remotely feel like it
right now, I wouldn't even know what for. I suppose
Ramiro would remind me that the same thing happens every time I take a trip, that then I don't want
to return, that I always get entranced with some
other life, that I fall in love with all those other wom-
en I am when I'm away, in other places, that what's
hard for me is commitment, that the alternative is
easy, that starting from nothing is always easy, and
I know, I get all that, and I don't feel like listening
to it, and besides, this isn't a trip. I don't know, spe-
cifically the feeling I have now is that nobody needs
me back there. They don't need me here either, but
something is broken, that's the sense I have. Now
I think I couldn't leave without first having talked to Julián, a little bit, even if it's just for a few
hours, just to have him talk to me, have him talk to
me about everything, tell me how he's doing, I need
to know, everything, maybe meet his kids? Maybe
even meet his wife? His pregnant wife? Would it be
wise to take that leap? Should I do that? Although
no, because it would be a kind of deceit, because I
want him too. And what would I even do there? I'm
going to just chat with—what's her name? Mariela?
Or was it Marianela? I don't know, I think my mind
is clouded from being so upset, I had an unpleasant
awakening, and I can't think clearly. I'd really miss
your cat too, if I left right now. And your parents.

I'm a wreck, I need a family, I want a family, and in some way, to a certain extent I feel like I'm usurping yours, even though I'm not, even though I know it's an exchange, and that I am obviously also giving something back, I must be, they've like adopted me. I feel like I can't return like this, the way things are right now if I leave, I'd be returning broken. I realize, I already am, I'm a little bit broken, but it wasn't the trip, I don't think it was that this time, I think I was already broken from before, that I'd been breaking for a while, which is why I came, or why I was able to come, by myself, too, because I could have come with Manuel, that's true, and I decided to come alone, which must be for some reason, there must have already been something that was broken. I can't leave like this, I can't, but I also can't stay. What the fuck am I going to do here? What the fuck am I going to do?

19.

I called my brother, in the end I couldn't help myself. I wanted to, I hoped to, my intention was to
get ahold of myself. I called myself to order, in
some sense. I knew he wasn't the person I wanted
to listen to, I knew I didn't want to listen to him,
and nonetheless, or precisely for this reason, I called
him. I think I kind of needed to be shaken or whatever by somebody who really knows me and is familiar—pun intended—with my self-deception mecha-
nisms. To my surprise, and kind of disappointment,
Ramiro wasn't that clear, nor did he go especially
deep with it. He basically told me to think, that's
what he told me, to just think about how I'd been
feeling. I explained it to him, I told him briefly about
my encounter with Julián and about how confused
I'd been and how upsetting I'd found the whole incident; he listened attentively, he asked me what about
Manuel, and I said, what about him? And he goes,
what are you planning on doing, and I go, what do
you mean what am I planning on doing, that's exactly what I don't know, I ask him if he's seen him,

if he knows anything, he says yeah, he saw him the other day and that nothing seemed to be up, he was normal, like always, that he'd asked him about me, if he had any news, since I was a spaz and hadn't even emailed him. And Ramiro had said yes, that he'd spoken with me, and that I was a little worked up about everything, which he understood perfectly, and that anyway I must be about to return. That re: today. Starting today, then, I ought to be returning, there's no more sense in my being here, I ought to be back on the road. So basically just that, that Ramiro understands my confusion, not that that really tells me anything, not that that helps me. He doesn't tell me what I might do about it all, nor does he tell me to stop it. He doesn't tell me to return, nor does he tell me not to. He just suggests I give Manu a call, even if just to reassure him, even if I don't really know what I want or whatever, but aside from that, you know, that I should just think about it, and take care. He tacks that on, take care, he just throws it in, and it's the thing that most sticks with me when I hang up. He also said Corsito is chilling, that he's gotten used to the house, that he's even taking certain liberties at this point. I hang up and realize I'm in the same place as before, that I have completely failed to move forward, that I have not evolved. That for god's sake someone please tell me what I need to do.

It's him who answers, when I call him at work. Hey, sweetie, he says, already yanking at my heartstrings. How's it going, he says, and he says how I kind of just disappeared, and he asks when I'll be getting in. Yeah, there's been a lot going on (me), with my dad, and your parents, and the ashes, the city, the south, the southern wind, the streets, the climate, or the atmosphere, I guess the atmosphere is what I mean. The scene. And the cold too, I mean. Oh, sure, of course, he can imagine, he had imagined, that he hadn't been too worried about that, that he knew I must be going through a lot right now. And when am I getting in. And I say, well, you know, I don't quite know yet, that I'm going to go get my ticket today, I'll have to just kind of see, that I'll let him know when I get it, but that things are kind of weird with me right now, just so he knows, like just so he's prepared or whatever, so he knows. That's fine, sweetie, don't worry, he says, that's what he says, that he'll be there, that he can't wait to see me, and I say me too, I want to see him too, and that as soon as I know I'll let him know, that's what I tell him, that I'll let him know as soon as I know. I love you, baby, he says, and I say it back. I miss you, he says, but I don't say anything to that. I'll let you know, beso, ciao. And take care, yet another take care.

I didn't say anything, I can't believe it. Such a coward. But it's fine that way too, I guess, in a way that's fine. What would I have told him? I wouldn't have even known what to say. Over the phone? And besides, what? I can't, it wouldn't be right to share my doubts with him. And over the phone. What would I say? That I mean I'm really sorry but I'm just kind of crazy right now because the other day

I ran into Julián, that yeah, that I hadn't seen him in years, and that as a matter of fact I hadn't even really thought about him when I decided to come here, that I had barely even remembered him, that he wasn't part of my life anymore, because he wasn't, because he'd ceased to be? Say that and then add on that now he was again, that now he'd come back up, that he'd come back into my life, just like that, and that I was letting him, that I was fully letting him come back. Say that and then say that that was why (that was the only reason) I didn't really know, I just couldn't really know right now what Juli's deal was, what he was thinking. So. That was that. That was it. Say, you know, Manuel, I adore you, and I really do care about you a ton, and maybe even that warm and fuzzy thing you make me feel, you give me, maybe love, it could be, I can't really know that, how could I? But whatever, there's also this other thing I wanted to talk to you about, this other thing I've been hiding from you, that I've been keeping, one that's practically under lock and key, or in a burlap sack—a bloody one, like a lump that's moving, writhing, that's having convulsions in rooms, in one-room apartments that are super saturated, and by greasy colors, dark red, dark green, maroon, like that, just like that, dark and mysterious, dull, dense, I have things inside of me that are moving. And when I pay attention to them a little bit they convulse and wake up and demand justice, demand I remember them. That bloodstained burlap sack, foulmouthed and stumpy, that doesn't want to be quiet and that

struggles and groans and grumbles when it feels
that I'm shedding any light on it, when it comes to
hear that someone's done something with that lock
and key, that someone's there. And meanwhile, I
could get out of there, lock it back up, step back,
and let things settle back down, or: pick the bag up,
untie its cord, release the beast, and let whatever
happens happen. Freeing the monster wouldn't offer me more than two possible fates: either it would
devour me or it would request my hand in marriage.
So, and since I don't know what I want, since I find
myself with my hand on the key in the lock, and my
eyes go from the bag to the well-lit room behind
me, which emanates warmth over my shoulders, and
from there to the burlap sack yet again, so I'd say if
you want to wait for me, like if you really feel like
it, wait and see what I end up doing with myself,
what I do with this, what I can do, what I'm able
to do, what I let win this time, or if I don't let anything win at all and actually make a decision this
time, to go for it, even if that going for it will lead
to destruction, even if it is destruction itself, but, in
any case, it would have been my decision. And if it
did go that way, if I stuck with the bag, the bloody
burlap, don't take it as a failure, don't take what we
had, or rather, the end of what we had, as the failure of something else, something bigger, something
grander, but rather as the success of itself: that long
vacation we took together when you loved me and I
loved you and nothing too terrible happened to us,
and nothing got too tarnished or anything, take it

as that, as what we had, which we liked and which was it while it lasted/which was everything, while it lasted.

I should have said all that to him, given I pretended to be fully sincere, and yet, no, it wouldn't have done any good, it probably would have only generated, first, a silence, finishing up with something along the lines of, oh, sweetie, I don't know, you're mixing me up now, why don't we talk when you get here? And he would have been right. So whatever, my problem, and I'm left alone with my images and to see how I'm feeling and what I can do about it. Which isn't much. For now I should, at least, be able to decide when to return.

20.

Before I leave I spend some time with Ali. We have a little love session. I pick her up and hold her in my arms like she's a baby, and she lets me, slippery though she may be, and hard though it may be for her to relax. I pet her stomach, put my head up to hers, rub up against her. She smells like roasted sweet potatoes, I don't know why, I don't know where she would have picked that up. But in any case, she smells good, I like the smell of roasted sweet potatoes, weird as it is that it's on Alicia, Alison. I can feel her purring, your cat doesn't make much noise, she doesn't purr externally, it's internal. But you put your hand on her stomach and you can tell.

It's strange, since I've been here I almost haven't thought about the past at all, it's super weird. I mean the distant past, my distant past. Ours, here, before. It probably has to do with the fact that absolutely everything here is so before that it would just be redundant. Or not, actually maybe not, since most people aren't actually here anymore, and those who are aren't recognizable, can't be identified with themselves, I mean, with what I remember of them. Maybe I didn't want to think about before because I wouldn't have been able to handle it: going to scatter your ashes from a bridge just into nothingness, into a landscape, thinking that was you, what you were. I guess a certain distance was necessary in order to go through with that and not completely fall apart, fall in with you. I don't know, I guess because of your parents too, to make things easier on them. And for me, for me too, of course, for me, too. Oddly enough now (and it must have to do with my impending return), after my talk with Manuel, with everything I didn't tell him about Julián and his family and his paternity and everything I also didn't tell him about your house with how the light hits it in the middle of the day and that nobody is ever here then, just your cat who smells like sweet potato and me, all this silence brings you back, materializes your presence, or your absence, or the fact that you're not here, your never being here again, so clear, so definitive. Then I think about the afternoons at the Percy or here in your room or in the living/dining and I kind of waver, I get weak. I realize, I think I realize that I want to leave, but I also know I want to take you with me, and it's impossible because you're here, very here, I just now fully understood that. From there, from Buenos Aires, I can miss you very contemplatively, look at you, at us, as though through a glass in a shopwindow, our common/shared past, behind glass, get into a funk about it but at a safe remove, removed by that window pane. There, on the shelf, there's a weak light that calms things down even further, and it gives it a halo of unreality, of something that happened far away and a long time ago, something one can step back from to observe, observe from afar, something one attends, as though it were something else, far away, removed from the body. But here it isn't like that, I get here and you're everywhere. In the cold, in the morning, in the pillow, in your jacket, in your mom. And you're outside, in the incline, the rubble, the asphalt, and right where the asphalt starts to be dirt almost imperceptibly, and you can't quite tell which one is eating up the other. There and in barking. In little dogs' barks, puppies of puppies of puppies. At the market, in the river, at the bus station. In weekend outings. In the teenagers. In the teenagers on the corners. On the curbs of the sidewalks. On the steps leading up to people's doors. In young couples making out. In that saliva, you're there, too. In the night and in the frost. In that chill and in the drop, precipitous, in the temperature when—right when—the sunlight stops. In the cars headed for the river, in naps when the sun's intense. In the rubber on the car window that gets overheated. In the arm that rests against that rubber and gets burned and tanned and has yellow hairs and sun splotches. In the legs over the imitation-leather seat, sweaty. In those drops of sweat that slide across the imitation leather and make those adolescent legs in a skirt or a pair of shorts stick to it. In the song that happens to be playing on the radio right then and sets the soundtrack for that moment. In the poplars that cast a little bit of shade along that river and on that car when it's parked in that one spot, right by the river and its little bed, its timid summer riverbed. In those adolescent legs, one, two, several, that stretch out over that river's rocks and let the water bump up against them but not cover them, the legs, the adolescents, but it does cool them off under that high noon southern sun that burns and overheats. In that wind that provides a little relief on the shore of that river, especially in the shade of those poplars, and it moves those leaves of those poplars and it makes them sound like rain. In the ears of those adolescents in the river, in the little trickle of the river, talking in half whispers, murmurs, because they are confessions, and the water transmits/transports the sound and they don't want to be heard by the other adolescents lying down in the shade of those trees. In the music that's still coming from the radio of the car and in those cigarettes of those adolescents who now rest in the shade of those trees listening to that music, even if it's not exactly listening, even if it's just the backdrop. In the adolescents who glance over at those adolescents in the current, adolescents with few clothes on, T-shirts, shorts, who laugh and tell each other secrets to the streaming of the water. In the scarceness of the clothing on that adolescent skin, tanned and exposed by the river, in the river, watched intermittently by those other adolescents in the shade of those poplars. In that and in the progression of desire. In its realization or suspension, in its coming to fruition or its utter frustration. In the back seat of some car, of that one or any other that looks like that one, in the shade of those trees or of others, in the afternoon or at night. In those kisses. In that languid sweat. In that ripping apart. Those tears, one or another of those tears atop one or another of those rocks or on the steps leading up to all of those houses, one of them, never one's own, never the same. In that ripping apart or in that pleasure, in the pleasure also taken from its being weird, new, different. In those tastes, in those smells, in those fluids. In those new fluids, different, foreign and one's own; parts of someone else's body in one's own, parts of one's body in someone else's. In that exchange, in the pleasure of that exchange or in that ripping apart. In closed eyes, in doing and in letting things be done. In wanting and refusing. In negation and advance. In disobedience and plundering. In plundering and in the pleasure of plundering, and disobedience. In those afternoons, those rivers, music. At the time of day when the skin starts to itch from the sun and from other things. The time of day when the sun was too much, and there's no going back, no undoing it, arms and legs in the water, brown, exposed to the sun. At the start of a chilly summer night, a cold that never goes away because it wouldn't dream of leaving, because it's from here, from this start of a night. In the attention paid to the start of a night that does not then occur, in that suspension they call sunset, although it isn't, let's not call it setting because it never really sets; in a beginning, at the start of something, let it not be night and let it not fall and let it not elapse and let it never go away, this, too, in this, as well; on that chilly summer night that won't ever end because it will not begin, because it's always just going to seem like it's beginning and not do it, and that way it will stay, as the start of a night that isn't and that won't be, no/ever, a night.

21.

People work, not me. I look out the window, look
out the window, out the window. Outside it's winter,
and it's sunny. The doors don't shut properly, they
don't shut, they're old. A phone rings through the
wall. How come it takes such daunting effort to do
what one likes? It's daunting, daunting to begin. I
find it daunting to get started, and that seems not
to be a fixable thing. The road to success, the road
to success. Who knows? I get tired of myself, I still
keep getting tired of myself. As pleasant as I find it
here, as pleasant as I find it. Did anyone pick up? In
any case, the phone stopped ringing. What works
better in fiction? Past or present tense? Weekends
make me cranky, I don't like them, that imperative
to have a good time, do things, do something special, the notion of free time. I prefer to seek out
those things while other people work. People relaxing tend to look ridiculous, like out of place, gro-
tesque. I'm unmotivated, a little, I realize, bored,
overly calm, almost comfortable. I don't like where
I live anymore, I'm fed up, I'm fed up with where

I live. I want, somehow, to live differently. I'd take care of it, I'd take care of that baby if he gave it to me, if he wanted to give it to me, if he wanted. I think I could be a good mother, I think so, I think I'd like to be a good mother, I think so. I don't know where my mind is, I don't know what I'm thinking about, I couldn't put it into words, couldn't specify, couldn't. I don't know what I'm up to, if I were asked what I was up to, I'd have no idea what to say, how to respond, what I'm up to. I know I get tired, every so often I get tired, I get exhausted and I no longer want what I had and want something else, something, something else. Waiting until the moment bursts, waiting until the moment bursts, what is that? Anxiety is never too good. At some point someone said it was the other side of despair, and I thought that sounded right. The backwaters abduct you, sometimes it's like a kind of barge that carries you away. Now my place in Buenos Aires depresses me a little. I haven't cleaned in months. I don't want to sleep in my room, I haven't wiped or dusted in months. Months. I want to get rid of all my books, all my CDs, most of all all the books I already read, why would I want them? I don't want them, I'd give them all away. I want to talk to people, I feel like expressing myself. With someone, with someone new, someone else, someone different, someone who might cast some new light on the situation. There are certain people I just stopped seeing and never ran into again and that's fine. I'm bored. Outside, in the city, there's the clamor that cities have, on Friday afternoons, the chaos of cities on Friday afternoons. Not here, here in some sense it's always the same time of day, the same day. There people come and go at full speed, in action. At full speed. While I, here, am quiet and tired, I get tired because I'm bored, I get tired when I'm bored and it makes me want to sleep, which is the only thing I want to do, is sleep. The same blocks, the same neighborhoods, always: the same thing that suddenly one day gives me a feeling of empowerment another day overwhelms me. I am me, that's my impossibility. There, once again, the only thing that can save you is fiction. I mean, whenever you can, when it gives you access. What isn't fiction consumes you. I don't want either breaks or obligations, although, obviously, I prefer obligations. I wouldn't know what to do without them. Live from event to event, as though it's nothing. Have kids to while away the time, even if that's all it is, to spend some time. Which is no small thing, spending time. I'm bored. I don't even know at this point what would be my idea of an adventure. I want to not want, not need anything. I already don't need anything, I already almost hate where I live, exclusively because I can't leave, that's already a good reason, I want to get out of there, I mean I'm almost never there anyway as it is, it's already mostly just a storage unit and a dust collector. I have to get it together enough to get to a different place, to be, to stay at, let it not be here, or yes, I don't know, try to understand where I want to be. Getting out of there is an imperative at this point, right?

And my books and my CDs I would give to someone, the new tenant, let them come with the house,
let them stay, let them lose their history, lose me, let
them stray away from me, let them forget me, with
no hard feelings, just do without me. I can't be there
any longer, I can't. Unconformity and comfort, everything all together at once.

22.

What a day, my god. It's done now, I'm going tomorrow. I'll leave you. I went to get my ticket, but I
didn't; something happened on the way.

I walk up Alvear perfectly calm, and just when
I'm about to cross, right in front of the station,
someone honks. I need to just stipulate, before you
jump to any judgments, that I had—I really had—
made a decision. I thought more seriously or took
a colder look, without so much stupidity, about my
relationship with Manuel, and about what we had,
about what we have, and I decided, I made a decision. That I don't want to lose him, that that, this,
is my life now, and that I can't just leave everything,
everything I have, everything that I've built in
whatever ways, for nothing. Because that's what it
is, because there's nothing, in reality, nothing else
for me, nothing awaiting me. Here, I mean, that's
what I mean, here. There is there, in Buenos Aires, I
think at the very least I made myself a space where
I belong that—as much as it tears me up to leave Esquel—I shouldn't take for granted. Because it tears

me up and will always tear me up, and it's not because of you, you know. Not at all, before you died it was just as awful or maybe not just as, I mean, it was different, but still terrible. Besides, your death isn't specific to a place, not at all, you're dead everywhere. So that, basically, I realize that it isn't wanting to escape, not at all, it's combating wanting to stay, because I would stay, I always would have liked to stay, I'll always want to come back, that's very clear to me, but it's also clear, I think, that's what I'm deciding, that it's precisely that distance, that tension, that sustains me. That desire towards that other thing. If I have it, I succumb. If I stay here, I succumb. I know that. Maybe, then, my doubts these past days have been nothing other than to succumb or not to succumb. Like with Julián, as though he were a mise en abyme of Esquel, or the reverse, as though Esquel were a mise en abyme of Julián, I don't know what order it would be in, but they're the same, in me, they're the same. If I stay, I die, it would tear me up inside, I know that, I'm aware of that much. It's a very strong drive, now I understand, I remember why I come so rarely, I get why it's so hard for me to come back, it's like vertigo, it has the logic of vertigo. And I would throw myself off, like you would throw me off, pull me down, like the girl in *Crouching Tiger, Hidden Dragon*. That's what it is, the death drive, the drive to be ripped apart.

So anyway, all that, that I had decided to return to Buenos Aires first thing tomorrow on the earliest bus I could take, at whatever time, to get there as soon as I could, to get on with my life. My life. That split is odd, speaking from here and referring to my life as though it were something else, as though it were happening right now in some other place, as though it were possible to return to life, to my life, to one's life. And I'm waiting at the light to cross the street and someone honks, a pickup honks and stops. It's Juli, it's Julián in the truck from the other day. He's not alone, on the passenger side, just sitting there loose like a little parcel, is the kid, his son, León. I can't believe it. The kid's closest to me. I go up to the window and he looks at me, the two of them look at me. Julián looks happy, surprised and pleased, he asks where I'm off to, if I want a ride, I say no, that I'm going right across the street, to the station, to get my ticket. You're leaving? he asks me, and I say yes, as soon as possible, that tonight or tomorrow morning at the latest, he asks me if I'm running away, you're trying to escape, he says, playfully, and I flash him a fake smile, as my only response, to his provocation. Is he yours? is the rhetorical question I then ask, and the child looks at me with eyes wide, brown eyes, light brown, just like Juli's, and his dad introduces us: this is León, this is Emi, Emilia, my ex, take a look at her, isn't she pretty? She could have been your mother. You're such an asshole, I say, wipe his face off, at least, you jackass, he's got snot all over him. I reach over through the window and wipe the snot off with the filthy bib the kid has on. I'm inundated with tenderness. I can't believe it and would like to avoid it at all costs, but I'm touched. So fucked up, maternal instinct or feminine instinct, whatever the fuck it is. Something like that desire to have stuffed animals, that's it, that stupid stuffed-animal sensation/need. Although it's not always, often I don't give a shit about kids, I mean I don't care about them any more than I do adults; there are a few I like and others I don't, like with anything, their condition neither exempts nor favors them. But this one in particular—I'm so predictable—I like. He's a little gruff, like Juli, I can tell. He looks at me suspiciously, and of course he's right. He scrunches up his forehead and watches me closely. Scrutinizes me. I say, hey kid, and he doesn't even remotely respond, he just stares at me. He's the exact opposite of a little demagogue. I like that. Soon enough, when he starts talking, he'll probably turn out to be just as sarcastic as his father. Captivating. Cute kid, I say, such a bad attitude. He does, he says, he has a really lousy character. He's also very aware of everything, says his father. I like him, I add. Do you want me to give you a ride? he asks, and I look at him askance, remind him where I'm going is a few feet away. No, no, he says, tomorrow at dawn I'm leaving for Trelew, I have to make a delivery, if it'd help I could take you. What would I do in Trelew? You'd take a bus. It's been ages since I've been to Trelew. I ask him if he thinks it's a good idea, he says he thinks it is, and it strikes me that it would be, that it is a great opportunity to have Julián all to myself, for the last time, probably, and to share a trip with him, with him and across the desert. But to be returning, at the same time be returning. I can't believe how fortunate and perfect the prospect is, it's been a while since anything has excited me this much. Okay, I tell him. And we agree that he will pick me up in the morning. I say goodbye to little León with a kiss on the forehead, he makes no sound, just closes his eyes, his head smells like things, a little bit like baby and another little bit like baby fluids, and a smidge like fried food. Give him a bath, dickhead, he smells like cutlets, I tell his father, and the kid looks at me with his eyes wide open, as though requesting I behave myself, as though demanding that of me. I'll see you, adds Julián, and he gets going. I wave goodbye, León responds by lifting up his little hand, he shakes it a bit and puts it in his mouth, his hand covered in dirt and snot.

Get a load of that, will you, a trip with Julián, in a truck, across the desert. Five minutes prior, one minute prior to that honking I was heading to the bus station to finish with all this, or, at least, to distance myself from it, or, at least, to put a safe distance between us, and now—boom—I find myself embarked upon a dangerous, attractive, not to say tantalizing, trip across the desert with the death-drive guy. A good opportunity to die, perhaps? Just crash the truck, and both of us could be smashed to smithereens, the two of us together on some torn-up road, blow a tire at full speed and flip over, hit some little animal at full speed and flip over trying to avoid it and not being able to, not being able to avoid it and plough right into it and have it smash

115

into the car, have it break the glass and come into the cabin with us, have it plough into us and disfigure us, because of the pressure, because of the weight of its body and the glass, to die, to die together and have them find us days later, many days later, maybe a family, maybe another traveler on a bus, a bus driver, torn apart and in the sun, half-eaten by vultures, half-bored-into by larvae, fly larvae that would have already nested in under our skin, taking us over? Nothing bad, a tragedy, two lives literally destroyed, that's what the papers would say, in Esquel, in Buenos Aires, two orphaned children, one of them about to be born, what a tragedy, and yet, destiny; those closest to us would understand that, the destiny thing, you would understand it, as much as you might disagree with this trip I'm taking, that I'm accepting, that I'm choosing, you'd understand it. You'd have no choice but to understand it. Of course, they died together, that's how it had to happen, such was their destiny, to rest together for all eternity. They'd need to leave us there, rotting in the sun, alongside a road in the desert, between Esquel and Madryn, so that order could impose itself anew, so that it would be restored, and becoming dust and spider food and worm compost, on the desert earth, which doesn't need us, which won't absorb us, fat, two stains of fat over infertile ground, dry, cracked, that would be good.

23.

I swing by my dad's to say goodbye. I have the wisdom not to mention anything about my plans, about the plan to destroy myself in the desert alongside Julián, because I have a visceral relationship with him, irremediable, impossible to live with. I don't tell him anything, I mean, I do tell him that Julián is taking me, that I do say, and even that's enough for him to glance over at me with an expression I know well, I've seen that face before, the *what are we going to do with you, Emilia* face, what are we going to do, and yet he knows, he knows I can't help it, he knows it's stronger than I am and he realizes—right now—that that has not changed. He asks, not without malice, and this is all he will say on the subject, if the whole family is going, or just the two of us. Another fake smile on my part, and a clap on the arm, for the audacity, for the perspicacity, for the degree to which his comment is appropriate.

24.

This one is a married couple around sixty years old. He has a serious *Psycho* face people would line up to see; she has a smile, a wig, shiny/new teeth. They smile, arms around each other, in all the photos. He buys a car to take her on a trip. A few days later—yet again, modus operandi—he says she has left, run off, with the car. There are witnesses who say they saw a suspicious woman with that same car, some ways away. The mysterious woman goes to an ATM, takes out money with her card, Denise's card, her own card, it's caught on camera, and there definitely is something strange about her. Her husband goes on the radio, begs her to come back, even if it's just for their grandchildren. In a plaintive tone he asks her to at least take pity on the grandkids. A few days later her family gets a goodbye letter from their mother, a suicide note. She laments in the card, says she's sorry for not having been able to be a good wife for George—the widower. A few days later someone finds the woman's sweater and her purse on the seashore. The hypothesis gets confirmed: suicide. But her daughter doesn't give up: she denies that the handwriting on the goodbye letter is her mother's, there's something there that doesn't quite convince her. So, they take the envelope and have it analyzed, the part you seal with saliva. And the DNA they find belongs to none other than George. They get him, and he confesses: he bludgeoned her and then he took her to his place of work and incinerated her in a furnace. All the rest was fake. And—of course—the mysterious woman who was seen in her car was just George dressed up as Denise/wearing his wife's clothing/wearing his Denise's clothes. It's strange that with that capacity for fiction he would have overlooked the envelope. Yet again the devouring thing, the swallowing thing, in the family. Everything kept in the family.

25.

I have dinner with your parents, just informally. I
didn't have time to let your sister know, so I said
goodbye over the phone; I think it was easier for
her to do it that way too. She even got a little bit
affectionate, I think she said something along the
lines of nice to see you or safe travels or take care
or something like that, surprising. I didn't even call
Vanina, I didn't feel like it, I'll send her an email
from Buenos Aires. I didn't feel like dealing with her
questions, or like evading them, either, I wouldn't
have been able to; and so I simply did not say goodbye. When I got home, to your house, it was already
nighttime. It wasn't too late, but it was dark out
already. I arrived with some provisions, a kind of
minimal gift for your parents. I got some nice wines
and some cold cuts to snack on, some of that prosciutto your dad likes. He still hadn't gotten there,
so I ended up chatting with your mom in the kitch-
en. She was washing some vegetables, I told her I
was leaving first thing in the morning, and she in-
stantly started putting together a farewell dinner. I

couldn't say no. I also wouldn't have wanted to. She said she'd gotten a couple of good veggies, really fresh, and she wanted to make a stew, so how could I say no? So I stayed with her in the kitchen, I asked if I could help, but she said no; in exchange she had me prepare her some mates and tell her what I'd been up to the past couple of days. So I told her the whole situation, the sequence of run-ins with Julián, the extent to which that had affected me, how unresolved it all was for me, the Manuel thing too, I also talked to her about Manuel, about the phone call, my confusion, the impossibility of knowing, of understanding. We talked about him and his kids, what your mom knew about it all. The overview that she gave was quite a bit less idyllic than I had imagined. She feels really sorry for them: Juli, the girl, the kid. I wanted to know why she'd feel sorry, and she said, well, that she imagined something else when she thought about a family, that Julián barely knew that girl when he got her pregnant, and that that girl was not at all prepared to be a mother, poor thing, she'd barely graduated from high school, and that is quite apparent, the body knows, that why did I think she'd have such troublesome pregnancies otherwise? The body knows, communicates, and if a girl that young can't have a healthy pregnancy it means something. That, you know, for the man it was different, that she saw Julián coming and going with the kid, when he felt like it, because he kept working, went on with his life, goes out, sees his friends, and meanwhile the poor girl spends her life in bed. That she isn't saying anything about him, that she thinks it's good for him to go about his life and all, but that you have to think things through more, that a child ought not to be a caprice, a pastime, or something to fill a void, to have something to do, that you just cannot be that irresponsible, that egotistical. That was it, that in some sense it's just egotistical because those children, those people, are new people, and you have to have something to give them, something with which to receive them, the best intentions at the very least, and actually not even. That even the best intentions aren't enough. That it makes her a little bit sad how unaware they are, makes her feel a little helpless. It did me good to hear all that, because in some way it demystified the whole matter and helped me remember what a burden fatherhood would be, all that responsibility and that permanence, what it means for there to be a whole new person. But on the other hand I also think, and I told your mother this, that a certain degree of unawareness is probably necessary in order to conceive, to have children. That, in some sense, it has to be a kind of game, because if you overthink it you'll never do it. And she said that yes, well, that maybe, but that in any case that young girl certainly was not able to enjoy being a mother, not even the pregnancies, because of being in bed all day, like a convalescent, as though the children or maternity sickened rather than fulfilled her, rather than being a fortunate event, bringing joy, and that she, personally, did not wish that for her daughters. For her daughters, she said, and immediately made a little gesture with her hand as though including me in that comment, including me in the daughters part, I guess, or at least in the maternity part. Then, as she put a lid on the pot where she was making the stew, she told me that as far as Julián went, in terms of what I'd told her about my confusion, my distress, that I try to just take it in stride, that I just enjoy the trip and seeing him after all this time. You two must have lots to talk about, a lot to tell one another, to catch up; she said I should enjoy that and not oblige myself to know, that was the main thing, that one never completely knows anything, that things, that events, ultimately decide for you, and that I ought to just let myself be. That I let myself be. Strangely that phrase always makes me think of letting yourself go, even though I know it's not really related.

And then your dad came, and we uncorked the wine and ate prosciutto and ate stew, and we still felt like a few rounds of dice. Your dad got out the Chivas and we sipped from our glasses, and the whole time Ali was curled up on my lap, the whole time we sat chatting after dinner. I felt like she could sense my departure. Or at least I liked the idea of feeling missed. Then your mom could barely keep her eyes open, so we said goodbye. They insisted on getting up in the morning to say goodbye, make me a coffee or something, some mates, especially your mom, and I kept saying no, that it wasn't in the morning, even, it was really first first thing, and that I wouldn't even want to have a beverage at that hour, that it was getting super late now and that I probably wouldn't even sleep, that they should just go to bed and not worry about it. They gave me hugs, it was very emotional, but like an exuberant emotion; your mom said take care, looking into my eyes, and immediately added, and have fun; your dad gave his classic little claps on the back, said to say hello to Ramiro, and as he was walking out he added, I'll be seeing you for a white wine again at Scuzzi. I laughed, said whenever he wanted, and they went to bed. I stayed there with Ali, me standing up in the kitchen, her lying down on the floor, stretching and considering/sniffing out what her next sleeping spot might be.

I decided that I wouldn't go to sleep. I was already too far gone, and I didn't feel like sleeping through my last few hours in Esquel.

26.

I got my bag ready, I didn't have all that much to put in it. I packed the Counting Crows CD, hope that's okay with you, and decided to take your jacket. Like to wear it out. Take it on me. I end up just hovering, and decide to go watch television. When I go to look for the headphones in the entertainment center so as not to bother your parents, I discover a discreet collection of VHS tapes, most of them recorded off TV, with movie titles written in by hand. Some in your handwriting, *Reality Bites*, for example. I can't believe that still exists, can't believe it could possibly have survived the hours and hours of exposure to which we subjected it. I thought we'd used it up, literally. But no. So then I knew what to do for the next hour and a half. At first the tracking had a little trouble, the tape started out with an episode of *The Simpsons*, one of the first ones, the one with Nanny Potts. Too bad, I could have happily watched that as well. Anyway, but so I put on the headphones, pull the armchair up, and Ali gets comfortable on my lap, not without first kneading me with her paws and claws, bumping up into the unconscious, into sleep.

So anyway, Winona Ryder and Janeane Garofalo are driving in their car, singing, provoking Ben Stiller, which is how it all starts. Ben Stiller! He did pretty well for himself there in the end, acting like an idiot, catching his dick on his zipper, getting into just about every scatological situation possible, in later movies. But this is the first one I ever saw him in, and I would go so far as to say it's the most dramatic role of his career. I remember I kind of had a crush on Ben, when I saw that movie, when we saw it back then, back when he was a thirtysomething yuppie. The one who didn't end up doing that well was Winona, who seemed to hold such promise. Didn't she? Or did she not? I feel like she got stuck in the nineties, like she just couldn't make the transition into the next century. Is there anything more nineties than Winona Ryder? There are probably a few other things, but without a doubt she'd have to be in the top ten. Poor Winona, now I see her and think she's overacting. But that was her thing, right? That was part of her charm. We all wanted to have her haircut and have it look as good on us as it did on her. In this she's great, I think it's the best thing she did. This and *Mermaids* and *Beetlejuice* too. But I'd take this one over those, she's gorgeous in it. In *Reality Bites*, Winona, you will always shine. And then there's Ethan, the most respectable of the three, I guess. He doesn't act in that many things, he tends to choose pretty good projects, he was married to Uma Thurman. In this one he and Winona are a lovely, horny young couple. There's some kind of youthful spirit there, fairly cheap, but effective in the end.

I don't know if the movie is good or not, probably not, but it doesn't really matter. The soundtrack holds up, it's still good, Garofalo is a great supporting role with her incredible voice, her baby face, and those bangs, and the movie has a couple of little gems that still work. Like that first dialogue between Ethan and Winona, walking around the city, with that little conversation of you and me and coffee and cigarettes and we don't need any more than that, something like that, and then the scene of them kissing, when they finally kiss, where she's wearing this highly sexy pajama-type outfit, and finally they kiss against the fridge, and it just kills you, that still works. And at the end, too, when he gets out of the taxi and is standing there in his brown suit, after shot after shot of Winona filling up ashtrays with cigarette butts and getting psychological assistance over the phone; he's there, she's there, they love each other, and that's it, they don't need any more than that, just having one another is plenty/enough. They're so hopeful. But sometimes, now, for example, that tonic hits the spot, that message of hope to think that love is enough, love, tobacco, coffee, and a few ideals, or not even, a couple of principles is plenty, no? Or at least in Houston in the nineties it appeared to work, right? I turn off the TV and there's not that much time left now before I leave. I go to the kitchen. I lift up Ali, who wakes up slightly but quickly gets situated again in the armchair. I ended up wanting coffee. And wanting to smoke. But I don't have anything to smoke, not cigarettes or pot. That's on Juli. So I put on some coffee—it smells incredible—and make a couple of salami-and-cheese sandwiches for the road. With mayonnaise for Juli, cream cheese for me.

27.

I'm ready. Before I leave for good, another little love session with Ali. I'm going to miss her, I feel bad leaving, leaving her. And not being able to explain it to her. Not being able to tell her why I'm leaving, or where I'm going. Or take her with me, for a while, like a divorced parent. Scheduled visits, the right to visit the cat. I sit back down in the armchair to enjoy her being there. She gets on top of me, makes a couple of rounds until she finds the perfect spot, the adequate curvature. She lets herself be pet, lets go. Suddenly she bites me. I get a little mad, but I understand. I know she knows. I know she can tell I'm leaving. So I let her get angry and manifest her anger. That's the right thing for her to do. I pet her in a very dedicated way, just like I would like to be pet if I had that much hair, and it works. The nice thing about it is that there can't be any speculation: I know that she will never be able to do the same thing to me, and that makes my gesture unconditional, and I like that it's like that, unconditional. We have our moment of love, the exchange is very intense, I lose myself in her, to her. I hear a horn, both of us are startled, and Ali, one more time, bites me. Such is our farewell. I take with me the marks of her teeth on my index finger. It's not nothing. Right away I hear a few soft knocks at the door. I run to the bathroom, look at myself in the mirror, I'm wearing your jacket, I don't think I look disgusting, I grab my bag, look around, and leave. Juli's at the door, sleepy looking, in his sheepskin. He greets me with an affectionate kiss on the cheek and a quick hug and grabs my bag. He throws it in the back, in the bed of the truck, under a tarp. Can you believe how cold it is? he says as I'm turning around to get in on the passenger side. I already feel nostalgic for Ali, it's awful, I feel like an abandoning mother, I'd love to kidnap her and take her with me, but I remind myself that cats are first and foremost creatures of place. Then I think, too, of Cora. I think about my mother, I'm linear, I said that. What would she have been feeling as she left it all behind? If I feel this way just about Ali, your cat, after a week's cohabitation . . . What the fuck could have been going through that woman's mind in order for her to leave behind—once and for all—a husband and two children? Two kids aged one and a half and three. Who could even remotely start to think of that? How? What the fuck came into her head or went out of it for her to just up and decide to move, to disappear/disintegrate like that? Could things with Dad have been that difficult? I wouldn't think so, based on how he remembers her; he never seemed to get too worked up about her or anything. Besides, Dad is not a violent person, that's very clear. Maybe it wasn't even anything that decisive, maybe it simply wasn't enough for her, something about us, the family package; something of what we gave her wasn't sufficient, wasn't enough, and so she left, one day she simply left. Cora decided to up and move. You decided to up and move, Cora, how. Maybe she hadn't even planned to leave and she went and she died, that could be, too, maybe she went to die far away, maybe she hid out somewhere in order to die in some other place, where our eyes couldn't reach her, far away from our gaze, like animals, like some little animals. For years I maintained that hypothesis: I couldn't bear the idea that my mother had left me/us to start a better life, or just a different one, because where would that leave us? I think we knew we were very charming children, no, that thought was too painful. So I preferred to maintain, for years and always keeping it to myself, the hypothesis that my mother had had the heroism to go die somewhere else, that she was suffering from, I don't know, terminal cancer, horrendous cancer that killed her little by little in some horrendous way, that gradually—maybe—deformed her, ate away at her, because of how the cancer was degenerated cells, and the only thing I could imagine as a photo of degeneration was something deformed, deformity; so she had wanted people to remember her as young and beautiful forever and had retreated to die with dignity and in hiding, in some other spot, in the mountains, maybe. For years I maintained, then, not only that my mother was dead, but also that she had gone to die elsewhere. I don't know why we never heard from her again, it's weird we never heard anything more from her. Lack of effort, I guess; on her part, on ours. Of course, once I'd abandoned the hypothesis of death at a distance, I had to come to terms again with the idea of the independent woman, the southern/Patagonian Nora Helmer who said I've had enough and slammed the door, all well and good in literature but a total shit show for whomever ended up on the other side of that door hoping for a little bit of love. Or a call, a letter, something. Or at the very least a death notice. Or a postcard from the Caribbean. Or a picture with another family, a new family, a foreign family, from elsewhere, and her with a new name. Like she'd started calling herself Greta or worse, something more Slavic, something Russian, with a bunch of consonants strung together, unpronounceable to us, and she had that, another family that was Russian, and she dressed like a Russian and was a communist. All that. I contemplated the possibility that my mother, by mistake, had gotten stuck on the other side of the Iron Curtain and had not been able to leave. She'd gone just on a trip, to get a little air, to clear her mind, taken a walk around Red Square (which in my imagination was in fact completely red, or red and white, I guess, with buildings like lollipops, like suckers, red and white, in a downward spiral), and when she wanted to return because she realized that she actually did want to live with us forever, they had closed the borders, and at that point she couldn't get out. And so she had become a communist. She'd ultimately ended up getting married to a Russian guy and having Russian kids, out of obligation, and she wore gray, everybody wore gray, everybody wore the same clothes, and they worked in factories, like robots, facing conveyor belts, with a kerchief on their heads, until a bell went off and they could go back to their homes, all identical, in silence, all alike. And then, every so often, a truck would show up with—for example—shoes, for everybody, or toys, and they were all always identical, all the shoes, all the toys, every shoe exactly like the next, every toy exactly like the next, so that there couldn't be any envy/in order to eradicate envy, so there wouldn't be any theft or any need to steal. That was communism to me, that was how I pictured it. That was how my mom was living, and she couldn't communicate, not even to send postcards because they didn't let you, because they checked all correspondence and if they discovered she had another family in some other part of the world, a double life, they'd chop her head off. So she had no other option but to live there, and her life wasn't that bad, just too identical to the lives of others. Then, at some point, I abandoned that hypothesis, as well, the hypotheses kind of just evaporated from one day to the next, as intense as they could be while they lasted. One day with no warning they would vanish, or change, like tastes, like so many other things. And every time I aborted one of those perfectly crafted theories, which didn't have a single hole in them and which permitted me to go to sleep at night, coming up with all kinds of new details for that other life (or death) of my mother's, what emerged again was the most awful hypothesis, the most painful one of all: the Nora hypothesis, the theory of the reckless independent woman, maliciously rebaptized in our adolescence as *let's just come right out and say it, Cora left us to go get laid,* or *Mom,* of course, that was also sayable. Obviously I never espoused any of these theories to our father, no señor, it wasn't something we talked about, it especially wasn't anything he ever brought up. There were pictures, though, of the two of them, in the seventies. They looked good, they looked great, they looked happy. The fashion of the times looked good on them. Dad was skinny and Cora was pretty voluptuous. I clearly didn't take after her; Cora is very Ramiro. I mean, the other way around. I turned out like Dad. Cora was from Buenos Aires, maybe she had gone back there. That is a very possible hypothesis and not even remotely interesting. During my teenage years Buenos Aires symbolized both everything I wanted most and everything I most detested. On the one hand I pictured it as ugly, jammed full of people all in a rush all the time. A clusterfuck of cars and taxis and buses and noises and people, and people, and people. In fact that wasn't altogether unfounded: we had gone on a trip there, just once, with Dad, to do some paperwork, some paperwork he had to go and do in Buenos Aires, and we stayed at our aunt's place, his sister's, who was living there.

Here. No, now it's there. And the memory I have of that trip, I don't know, I must have been about five years old, is of crossing Libertador in Retiro (now I know where it is, in my memory it was just a big avenue), and trying to get to the other side around everybody's legs, through all those legs, hundreds, coming towards us, ready to trample me, like a stampede; it was get across or die trying, and at the same time not lose Dad's hand, not let yourself get tricked by some other hand and end up who knew where. That crossing generated an extreme mixture of terror and adrenaline in me; the terror, the adrenaline, sufficient for me to insist to my father that we go again, more than once, cross that forest of legs in motion, all furious, all enormous, all going in the opposite direction. You might say that image illustrates quite well the configuration of Buenos Aires in my head: that excitement, that fear of losing, of being lost, of dying, literally trampled/crushed, and, nonetheless, the challenge, the challenge of avoiding it, of surviving all those knees wrapped up in suits, in stockings, of beating those heels, those soles, those purses and briefcases, and making it— unscathed and holding on to someone's hand—to the other side. Now that I think about it, my perception of Buenos Aires hasn't changed all that much, it's just that in this version my knees are at the same level as the rest of them, and my head is much higher, and some part, some little part, of the city, meanwhile, now belongs to me, as little as it is. I think that something of the apartment where we live, in the meantime, does belong to me. Doesn't it? Something, a piece of the wall, of the floor, of the wood on the floor, a dish, something. I think at this point some portion of that apartment must be mine.

Then, when I was a teenager, I wanted to know about Cora. For real, know for real. As a teenager, I asked. I asked for real. Dad didn't know exactly, but he knew quite a bit. He even had an address, in case something came up, in case one of us wanted to know. Dad gave me Cora's address, she was living in the United States. Dad had always had that address, just in case, in case of something literally life-or-death. Until then the only serious information that I'd gotten as a response to my childhood questions had been that my biological mother had had to leave and hadn't been able to come back and that she wasn't ever going to, either, but why? Because. As a teenager I needed to know. That my mother wasn't dead, I think that—in reality—I'd always known that, no one had ever held the reverse, except for me. Except me, when at school I'd been asked about my mother and I'd said I didn't have one, that I was an orphan, like those people on soap operas, there was always some easy reference to make there, an orphan like those girls, tragic suffering figures with romantic destinies. I think that in some moment I'd ended up convincing myself it was really like that. But it wasn't, and Cora lived in the United States, in New Mexico or somewhere. It wasn't really that easy to find her either, because she didn't exactly have a home, or she did, maybe it was a home, but not a house on a street, but one in some weirder place. Once, when I was a teenager and wanted to know, I wrote a letter to Cora, a letter. I wrote it and sent it in the mail, a letter to the United States, from Esquel. A letter from me to a mom, my mom, but who didn't want to be my mom. In the letter I put that it was me, that it was Emilia, her daughter, and that I wanted to know how she was doing and that if maybe she had anything to tell me she could tell me it, that she could write me. It took Cora a long time, a very long time, to write me back. Or her letter took a long time to arrive. By the time it got there I wasn't expecting it anymore. So I received it with quite a bit of skepticism and resentment. The letter was very short and written in very lousy Spanish. That mother, it was clear, no longer had any mastery of our language. Her letter was neither encouraging nor discouraging, it was evasive. She said she was happy to hear from me and to know I was well. That that wasn't exactly her address, but that I could write to her, that she'd be pleased to receive my letters. That her life had started to be luminous at last and that New Mexico was her place— she said it in English, not *Nuevo*, but *New*. That she could tell that I was a sensible person who had my life together, that I was prepared for life. That that filled her with joy. And that she sent her blessings, to my brother and my father and to me, that my father was a good man, that I should know that. And she said for me to have a good life, and *hasta siempre*. So nothing concrete about her, who she lived with, if she'd had another family or not, and what was the "luminous" thing. Nor did she want to know anything concrete either, nor any remorse, nothing. Pure nothingness. A kind of flash of a mother that wasn't even a flash, a little cut of light, a sensation and nothing more, just silence again. Nothing motherly. And you know, I didn't cry that much, we did those parodies of a hippie out-of-it mother, but the pseudohippie, unaware hippie, superfluous hippie, Cora and her tulles, Cora and the luminous light. Then, when I was older, returning to it, Dad gave me to understand that she had always been depressive, and a little out of it, and that apparently motherhood had not agreed with her, that in some way she had plunged into a crisis and hadn't been able to manage it. That after my birth she had gotten fully depressed, that she had a girlfriend in New Mexico who'd invited her to come for a vacation to get herself together and rest, and that Cora just hadn't ever come back, resolving and freeing herself from everything, from her former life, by letter and by phone. How do you like that? Poor Cora, like that, better to lose her than to find her. And Dad with the whole song and dance of the kids and the abandoning wife, one with her maternal instincts askew, what do you make of that? I can't judge her, nor do I want to, she's out there somewhere in her tunic in the desert on horseback, riding bareback, braiding leather, or working in a gas-station store, who knows. Leaving me defenseless, but what can I do about that?

28.

It's still dark when we head for the highway. I want this moment, I realize that. Everything about this moment makes me want it, makes me like it, even the cold: getting on the highway first thing in the morning, having a mate kit at my feet, ready to be prepared, the cookies in the same bag, the road across the desert, Julián's company, his nearness, being enveloped in your jacket, resting the nape of my neck in the hood against the leather, the imitation leather of the seat, the fog on the windows, the music, the music we're going to be able to listen to, all those songs. And talking, being able to talk to Julián and maybe not doing it, being able to decide not to do it, that, too. Filled with possible things, that's what I feel, that's how I feel right now. All around me, windows upon windows. And on the other side of the glass: Esquel, the mountains, the morning, dawn, and soon, nothingness, the total void, a total void, with morning, with sun. For the first while we sit in silence. We stop, get gas, Juli asks me if I need anything, I'm only barely capable of saying no, of saying it by just shaking my head. He goes in and pays, comes back and presents me with a little umbrella candy. Thanks, I say, and I put it in the pocket of your jacket. Your jacket, ours. Juli starts the truck and goes around the roundabout, and now we really are, we really are on the road now. He tells me to choose some music, I answer that I'm still good without it, that for now I'm fine with silence, whether it bothers him to stay like this a little longer, without music, and he says no, that that's fine, but that in that case could I prepare some mates for him because otherwise he'll fall asleep. Of course, how could I resist this, it's exactly the right time for mate, it couldn't be more appropriate. I try to prepare it as decorously as possible, omitting the gesture of getting rid of the dust; it wouldn't be good for our heated cabin, the volatility of the dust of mate. I add a little sugar to the first one, because of the acidity, and I drink it. Juli doesn't like sugar. It's a good moment. I know without needing time to pass, without needing the future, meaning distance in time, to lend it value, resignify it: I know now. I offer the mate to Juli, and the color returns to his face. He tells me he could barely sleep, I couldn't sleep for shit, he says. Apparently the kid spent the whole night screaming. He didn't want you to leave, I say, a little bit in jest and a little serious, and I tell him how Alicia bit me. I show him my hand. Who's Alicia? he wants to know, and I tell him, I tell him it's your cat, doesn't he remember, can he really have forgotten, and he asks if that cat's still alive. It's not a hamster, cats can live a decent number of years, to please not be such an ignorant brute and he says, it's basically the same. What's basically the same, I want to know, and he says, basically the same, Alicia and my son, he's being sarcastic, I realize now. He gives me back the mate, I add more hot water. I drink this one. No, it's not the same, obviously, that Ali doesn't tie me down or anything, and that I didn't sleep at all, either, but that it was because I didn't want to, that's another difference. What did I do, he wants to know, and I tell him how I watched *Reality Bites*, he wants to know which one was that, we saw it a million times. The one . . . that one where she leaves the guy, the musician guy for that dickhead-looking yuppie, what was that guy's name, the really funny one? Right, that one, I remember now which one it is, the one where she's filming a movie, and when she goes to see it it sucks because that yuppie of hers had sold it and their faces are on pizza slices, and she gets upset, I add that part, yeah, that one, he asks where I came up with that, and I say it was just there, at Andrea's, and I prepare him another mate. Meanwhile we're leaving Esquel behind, just like that, nothing more, without trouble or fanfare. So I ask him, then, if he gets away a lot like this; do you get away a lot like this? I ask him. Like what? he wants to know, like this, you know, get away from your old lady, I say. You're such a bitch, don't call her my old lady. Why not, she's your wife. Fine, call her my wife, then, if you want to, but don't call her my old lady, it sounds atrocious. Plus she isn't mine.

Wow, how modern. You're such a shit, he says. I add more water. For myself. I make some noise with the metal straw. I see that I'm going to have to switch up my strategy. The thing about the wounded pride doesn't suit me anymore, I am aware of that. I'm going to have to get myself back together. Otherwise this trip won't end up being very interesting at all.

Did you get married because you wanted to or because you thought it was the right thing to do? I ask him, not looking at him, as I pass him the mate. We both stare straight ahead, both looking at the road. He doesn't talk. He's thinking. I don't know, he says after a while, she wanted to get married, her family is very conservative, and there wasn't that much of an option, we were going to have a child, so I mean it was already kind of the same thing, anyway, in any case it was a really small thing, just for family and very close friends. That's so intense, I say, I never would've thought you would get married, or maybe I did, but not so young. Or at least not with someone other than me. You didn't want to get married. What does that have to do with anything? is the only thing I can think of to respond. I wouldn't have, says Julián, thought so either, but that's what happened, it just happened, I don't know, and now here I am. So intense, I repeat, as I push the metal straw around, and I realize that that's my default phrase whenever I don't know what to say, whenever I'm perplexed about something, *so intense*. I want to go more in depth; I can tell he's amenable, and I want to go into more depth. It's a good opportunity, and it isn't only that: I really want to know. Are you in love? I ask him. The heavy artillery, he says, and I say, let's just start with the hardest stuff, get the worst out of the way, that way we can relax for the rest of the trip. I need it, I clarify, I need to know. He says, okay, and he thinks. And drinks mate. I wait. And look, look out the window, at the landscape. It's been many, many years since I've been on this road. I'm not even sure that I ever came through here. Actually, I did, once, with my dad, but we were traveling at night, by bus, and I don't remember anything. I don't know, I care about her a lot, says Julián. She's very fragile, he concludes. Right, I say, closing my fist over the lid of the thermos yet again. That always sells well, fragility. Well, a lot of people buy it. I guess. But you get along well? Yeah, she's very laid-back, Lala, you can't not get along with her. Is that a good thing? I don't know, I think so. I don't think about that, I mean she's the mother of my child, of my children, that's that. Stab. Sure, let's say that's that, I think, but I just say, sure, and add, partly trying to conceal it, partly to give myself a little breathing room: You mind me asking? No, he says, and neither of us says another word.

29.

I don't want to ask any more questions. Now for a while I don't feel like doing it anymore, like asking. We drink mate, for now we focus on drinking mate. He doesn't seem surprised that I stay silent, that I don't keep asking him questions, just when he's set me up for that, to want to know freely. But it's a question that I asked out of bewilderment, from a place of bewilderment, and now I don't want to go any further. Or else I just can't, it's probably that I can't. I'm left with everything he did tell me, everything he affirmed. It's strange: I'm not relieved he's not in love with her; or am I? No, because it's not like that means he's in love with me. Because I don't even know how I feel, what I would want. And because all of this is ultimately a big stupid waste: who loves whom. It would seem to be more mixed up than that: it would appear that no one knows exactly who loves whom, if indeed anybody loves anyone, if indeed anyone understands, knows, or has a clear idea of what it is to love, or of what love is. Which is horrific, there's clearly something very wrong here, something I am obviously doing wrong. Or judging, judging wrong. He says he isn't in love with her, that is clear to him, hence I can infer that he knows what it means to love someone, or knows what love is. And he clarifies he cares about her. And that he has kids and has a lifelong commitment (even if it's just via the kids, which isn't nothing) to this other person. This person— he says—he does not love, but rather cares about. Perhaps love is unnecessary, that's another thing. Perhaps romantic love, like that, in those terms, the soul mate and all that goop is nothing other than a movement towards, but always from afar. It's not that bad, all in all, that he keeps a distance, that he always keeps his distance. Who really wants to have and hold and all of that? Nothing compares with wanting. Having itself is nothing, let's just agree on that. In sum, what more can I say? In this sense I'm in the best moment of my relationship with Julián: I don't have him, I'm never going to be able to have him, he doesn't belong to me, and, nonetheless, here we find ourselves, sitting next to each other, looking in the same direction, ahead, at the highway, at the desert, and—farther up—at the ocean, too, behind a pane, the landscape behind a pane of glass and us moving into it, moving in its direction. What more can I say? Counting Crows, of course, is what is coming. I'm in a good mood, in a happy place, in a profoundly, fundamentally happy place, I'm here and it's now and this is, very clearly, the best place to be right now in the whole world. The first chords of "Round Here" start up. *Tralala tralala tralala, tralala tralala tralala . . . Step out the front door like a ghost into the fog where no one notices the contrast of white on white. / And in between the moon and you the angels get a better view of the crumbling difference between wrong and right. / I walk in the air . . .* What was that? Julián interrupts me. I ask him if he's kidding, he says no, that it sounds very familiar, and he makes that little sound, like of pain, and makes a gesture with it, that little painful sound of knowing, of having it there somewhere, of being able to tell that you know and nonetheless not being able to recall what it is. Counting Crows, jackass, I say. No, he says, a no with a very extended *o* to it. I say yes, and I also tell him I found it in your room, half-hidden, that it had been years since I'd thought about it, about this album, that the past few days I'd been listening to it a lot. It wasn't their best, right? he says, oh, I don't know, I say, I can't be very objective, that for me it has to do with more than just its quality as music, that I can't really evaluate that. And I add that this song is awesome, that "Round Here," which is still playing, is amazing. It's good, he says, and he asks me if it wasn't in the music video for this song where the singer was walking along these tracks, that he was singing on some tracks in a leather jacket and like these dreadlocks. I tell him I don't remember that, but that I do remember other images from the video, of an esplanade, a salt flat, and this crazy woman, this girl with this suitcase, but that yeah, it probably was, because the guy, the singer, had dreadlocks. He tells me he also remembers that he was doing something with his hands while he sang, something unusual, but he's not exactly sure what it was, but he feels like he remembers that. I don't know, maybe, I say, and I put it on again, start it from the beginning, so we can listen to it. During the intro I say it's a good CD to listen to on the road. And then we fall silent, for the rest of the song. Outside the landscape has gradually lost its greenness, has desertified little by little, and the mountains have retreated into the horizon, and, ahead of us, the steppe. A great synchrony: this song and the landscape. If we stopped and I got out of the car with my stuff I could be the crazy woman with the suitcase, but with a backpack, a matter of details. Then, right around the second song and after saying that this one, the new one, doesn't seem as good to him, Julián tells me that León loves music and that it really calms him down. I say I've heard that, that people say that, that kids really like music. Cats, too, cats really like music too, it relaxes them, if it's soft music, obviously. As soon as I finish saying it I recollect myself and realize I've done it again: again I have compared his son to a cat. It's the best I can do, I guess, it's the most similar thing I have. In any case, he doesn't dwell on it, and he tells me, smiling, that what León really loves is reggae. I laugh, I mock him by telling him he probably didn't give the kid much of a choice. He tells me Lala (how I hate hearing the nickname) puts on a lot of other stuff for him too, music for children or classical music, and it's not the same, the little guy keeps crying. That, on the other hand, reggae always works. He's pleased, he seems to be something like proud. It's touching to see him like this, and, at the same time, it makes me nauseous. I ask him if it doesn't scare him, he asks what, I say having a kid. Scare me how? Oh, I don't know, just scare you: scare you that something might happen to him, or just the responsibility you have, that you guys have, as parents, I don't know, as adults, as people responsible for someone else's life. He thinks. After a while he says he doesn't know, that he never thought of it like that. That when I say it like that it sounds terrible, like taking out a loan from the bank or something like that, like being arrested, like having sold your soul, like a punishment. That it doesn't seem that bad to him. I tell him it's not that I think it's bad, but it does seem transcendental/definitive to me. Yeah, he says, yeah, it is, but that as far as that goes it's definitive in a good way, and that, like everything, once the kid is there it stops seeming so monumental and starts just being there. The kid's just there, he says. That's what he has to say. That it's not that big of a deal, that you don't stop being you. I add that, nevertheless, in some way, you kind of divide in two. I mean, he says, I don't know, I guess I don't know what you mean by divide in two, and then I'm the one left thinking. These are actually all just speculations, that's what I think I think, and that's what I say, and I add, too, that like I look at him and look at him with this, this other person who's like him but like a miniature version and that—the last time I saw him—that other person wasn't there, because he didn't exist. That that to me seems amazing and miraculous, a miracle, and not in the happiest of meanings. In what, then? asks Juli, in what what? I say, in what meaning. I'm not sure, I mean, I really don't know, I guess in more of a surprising or surprised meaning, like in the most dumbstruck, flabbergasted way. He's quiet for just a second, and then he wants to know what exactly flabbergasted means. Idiot, I say, and I punch him in the shoulder. Immature, he calls me, and he pushes my head with his right hand. He's looking straight ahead, driving. Can we talk for a while about something other than me being a father? he asks, and I remind him that he was the one who started it, with the cute little anecdote about his Rastafari kid, he admits this and insists, then, that we declare a truce for at least an hour or so, just for a while. I clarify that I like talking about his son; he says, so do I, but not only and not all the time. And he says he wants me to talk too, that he wants to know about me. What do you want to know? I don't know what to tell him, I don't know if I should be honest, I don't know if I feel like it. The last time he asked me if I had a boyfriend he didn't really want to hear the whole answer, it was enough for him just that I said yes, just the fact, and then he didn't want to know anything else. I don't want to expose myself to the same situation again. What do you want to know? I don't know, what you've been doing for the past five years, for example, I don't know, whatever. I don't know, like when you ask that I don't know what to tell you, I don't know where to begin. Are you happy with your boyfriend? he wants to know. A completely impartial listener, of course, this is not tendentious at all. What a question, I tell him. Yes, I'm happy. I mean, happy, I don't know exactly what you mean by happy, you know me, I'm still me, but yeah, we get along well.

"Are you in love?"

"I don't know. I was thinking about that a minute ago, when you said how your wife, Mariela—her name is Mariela, right?—how Mariela is someone you care about but aren't in love with or you think you're not in love with her and you said it just like that, with such clarity, and I started thinking about that, how you can have that much clarity regarding that, regarding how you feel."

"So you're not in love, then."

"Why not?"

"Because if you don't know, it's a no, you wouldn't hesitate."

"That's ridiculous, it's very naive, I think everything's much more complex than that."

"I don't think so."

"So then why the fuck did you get married to a girl you just like or kind of care about?"

"Because that's how things worked out."

"That kind of determinism is disgusting. You can't do anything about your life, you don't make decisions, you just let things happen?"

"I guess so, yeah."

"Well, I think that's horrible."

"That's not the most important thing, that's an immature argument."

"What?"

"The argument that you can only choose someone or build something with someone if you're in love, what the fuck is that? It doesn't work like that, there are a million other things, other factors."

"You literally just told me that people know when they're in love."

"Exactly, but what I'm saying is, that has nothing to do with anything."

"How does it not?"

"It just doesn't. Like you saying you were in love with me but still going off to Buenos Aires."

"What does that have to do with anything? That was because of something else."

"That's exactly what I'm saying, it's not the only thing, then, it's not the determining factor; for you, in that moment, it wasn't enough."

This stops me, I shut up. I don't know what to say, I can't rebut this, I can't rebut anything. I wonder, I wonder then if it's true that it wasn't enough, for me, back then. Probably not, or it was, but it wasn't important enough at that time. I had to live my life, and to do that I needed to go to Buenos Aires. I had to live my life, and to do that I needed to go to Buenos Aires.

"I was your life back then, or at least a part of it, and you left to find another life, in some other place."

"Don't be like that, Julián."

"Like what?"

"So difficult."

"I'm not being difficult, stupid. I'm not saying it because I'm holding a grudge, I'm being cool about it."

"Being cool about it, fuck you."

A little strain, but at least we laugh about it. I'm kind of depressed now. He asks me to switch the music. He tries to look through the glove compartment; he can't look and keep driving, he asks me to look for the Babasónicos CD. Which one do you have? *Dopádromo*, I think, and *Trance Zomba*'s on there, too. A good selection. I applaud him for compiling it. I put it on and put it on shuffle; I want "Montañas de agua" and "¡Viva Satana!" to come on as soon as possible. And I want them to surprise us. It starts off with "Ambush." What crafty things, these shuffles. In any case "Ambush" is perfectly fine. Juli says, let's stop in a bit to eat something, I tell him I made sandwiches. He says then let's stop to eat the sandwiches, that he doesn't like to eat while driving, that then he feels like he hasn't eaten. I like the idea of a little picnic by the side of the road. What kind of sandwiches? he wants to know; don't worry, I put mayonnaise on them, I do remember some of what you like. I'm hurt, I realize, but I don't want to share that with him. All in all, it's not entirely his fault. In fact what he said is true, and it's not like his tone was particularly hurtful. We were having a conversation, laying out our arguments alongside one another, and he ended up being right, what can be done. But is he, ultimately, right? Or did his tone just make me think that? Let us see. That love is not enough, was what he said, I think. Or that it doesn't matter, or that it's beside the point. He also said, as evidence, that I said I was in love with him and that I left all the same, left him. This is true in some sense and not at all true in others. I left, that's true, but I didn't leave him. He could have come along. And he didn't want to. Or couldn't. Meaning that either he wasn't as in love with me as he said or—and here we get back to the crux of it—love is not enough/love is insufficient/love gets you nowhere/love leads to nothing. I was in love with him, I was, I wouldn't even maintain that I'm not any longer, and yet I decided to go and live far away from him. I didn't give up other things for his sake, on the contrary, I went away from him towards those other things, all of them uncertain. I had a life and a possible future life in that place, and a different life, an unknown life, in another place. I opted for the latter, I opted for not knowing. I went towards the uncertainty. And then I opted not to go back to think about whether or not I was in love with him and whether or not it was enough or if it was a one-way street on which you had to either make a choice or make a choice. At that time I thought that if I stayed, a few months more would have killed us. Literally. Or worse: everything would have dissolved. I thought I had to go to college, I thought I had to get far away to—to be better, to be different?—to see other things, to meet people from other, many other, places. I couldn't (I wouldn't) give that up. And he wouldn't (or couldn't) give up his aversion to the city, to the big city. And that was stronger than us, because it was an us, that was what we were, but each of us on our own, as individuals, no longer together. And so it went: and so we didn't. The worst is that now I can't even tell which one's better, what is for the best, what would have been best, to leave or to stay, stay with him or not stay with him, if Manuel, if what. It's probably all the same, that's the point. Now I don't even know. How depressing. If love isn't enough, what's left? I always thought—at least with this—that it was something you could believe in. So many books, so many movies where everything is solved with love, by means of love. Where love is the saving grace. And here, in the real world, it neither saves nor is even sufficient. It's just another thing, like an accessory, an adornment, something that embellishes but that could—easily—not be there. Love as ornament, what do you make of that? As ornament. So depressing. So then, what difference can it make at this point if it's Julián or Manuel or whatever, if in any case it's nothing more than a contingency and will never be enough? He asks if I'm depressed now. No, no, nothing's wrong, I lie, and it's only then that it sinks in that "Montañas de agua" is just ending. Who cares, I'm depressed, what difference will a Babasónicos song make, who can drag you out of the mud of not being in love, of the absence of love, or worse, of its futility. I keep my mouth shut, I stay quiet, I opt for silence and float around out there, on the other side of the window. Such sadness, such nothingness.

30.

A sadness dream, without ambitions, that's what it
is: a dream with no ambitions. A recurring dream,
then, strange, because it has continuity. In time. Like
a kind of recurrence that nonetheless advances in
time. At some point, in some other unconscious moment, I cut a boy into pieces, it didn't matter that
much who, some kid from school, from a lab, something along those lines. At some point in a previous
dream, another—I remember neither how nor why
at this point—I killed him and cut him up into pieces. Now and since that time—here we have the sense
of continuity—I carry him in a bag. In a sack. Like
a burlap sack, one like that. At this point it reeks,
that's the primary problem. I need urgently to get
rid of it. I'm not worried about the death of the boy,
I'm not upset about the crime in itself, there is no
guilt. What does terrify me is having in my hands
the element of the crime, the cadaver. In the dream,
then, and constantly, I'm trying to figure out how
to get rid of it. I do think the best option would
be to burn it, but I can't find a way to do that. So I

think of sinking it somewhere, but I also can't think where, and I also am afraid it will float back up again somehow. On this occasion I'm traveling by car with the bag, someone is driving me, it's odd, my sense is that the driver is death itself. But they're not. I'm afraid the smell will be noticed. I get dropped off at school, it's a different building, of course, more rural, the dream one. I get dropped off. There are a lot of people around. All carrying things. I'm very upset. What deeply terrifies me is that I'll get found out and taken to jail. That's what scares me: losing my liberty, that above all, losing my liberty. Having perpetrated a crime doesn't strike me as all that problematic, being found out and put in prison does. I deeply fear this; I fear that on the bag and on the pieces of the dead boy they'll find my fingerprints. I leave the bag in the hallway along with others, other bags of other students, bags, things, and I move away. When I go back, later, the bag isn't there. None of the others are, either. I'm afraid. I can't figure out if the other students took it or if the trash people came by. I'm afraid. I think how if anyone came across the remains the path to me would be very direct.

I wake up.

Babasónicos are playing, it is what it is. I can't connect much with that now, not as much as I'd like. Around here, a little ways up, there's a place with a tree, a tree by itself, very odd. Let's eat there, he says. I say okay, he asks if I'm okay. Are you okay?

he asks, I lie and say I am. The sun is very intense over our heads, on the roof of the truck. I took off your jacket some time ago. I like this heat, the heat of the sun. I see, then, a few feet ahead of us, that tree. Julián points there, to our right. He slows down, and we get a few feet off the highway, on the side of the road, because there isn't any shoulder. We roll up in the truck to the tree, which is, or at least at this moment, rather scrawny. But it's also really quite pretty, quite nice to see, kind of curvy on one side and with strange foliage on the other, as though split in two. A little like the baobabs from *The Little Prince*. A little bit like that. I don't know if the image I have in my head is from the book's illustrations, from what I imagined, or from the movie, but what I know about baobabs, what I recollect of them, resembles this. Juli tells me he doesn't remember at all. I say, did you not read *The Little Prince?* and he says yes, but I can't remember everything, hon. *Hon*, he says, how sweet, how anachronistic. That nevertheless he does remember very well the elephant that gets inside the boa constrictor, that the rest, the adults, saw as a hat while in reality it was something else: a snake that had gobbled up an elephant, a boa constrictor with an elephant inside it. Oh, yeah, I loved that part too, but even more, the thing that I loved even more than that or anything was the part where the boy asks the aviator to draw him a little lamb, or a little sheep, and the aviator tried but kept failing, the Prince wasn't satisfied until the guy sucked it up and drew him a box, a cardboard box, with holes in it and told him how inside that box was his sheep, and then the boy was happy because he could imagine it however he felt like. And this spot, our picnic spot, was something in between the baobabs and the aviator's desert, that place with dunes, where the aviator drew the boy the little box. So we eat beside the truck/plane. It's cold here, even though the sun is beating down. In the air there's something cutting, a cold, in wind form, not that strong, because it's noonish, but persistent, meaning I zip up your jacket and everything. And the sun is very welcome. I think that the dryness of our surroundings, the sharpness, the inclemency of the sun, and, of course, the sandwiches do away with my melancholy. The steppe, in a couple of seconds, dissipates my sadness, evaporates it, as though it had dried it out, like a raisin, me a raisin girl of sorts. We eat standing up next to the truck, we move around as we eat, standing still would be freezing. I like this place, I compliment my traveling companion on his choice. Good, he mutters at the end of a big bite of sandwich, I always saw it from the road, one time I stopped to take a picture, of the tree, but it was late, and I couldn't take the wind. So really this is the first time I've stopped. How'd the picture turn out? I ask him. I don't know, I haven't developed it yet, he says, that's right, I say, you never develop anything, what do you take them for, it's amazing you still feel like taking pictures. These sandwiches are good, he says. Thanks, I say. There's something déjà vu, he explains, about this place, it always gave me that impression, since I discovered the tree, since the first time I saw it: it gave me this sense that it was a place I had already been to, that I had already encountered. But do you always go by here? I interrupt him. Yeah, he says, but he'd never paid attention before, and then one day he saw it, as though for the first time, and he could have sworn he'd never seen it before, that this tree hadn't been here. There. So it was that, that going by there, by here, ever since that time, had given him the strangest sensation, of belonging, in a strange way, of this being his. I say that maybe it's what I've been saying, that it's a place that resembles others, that makes you think back to other places and that perhaps because of that he thinks he recognizes something he doesn't really. Because, besides, even if he thinks he hasn't seen it before he always used to go by here, so he probably already had that tree in his retina, even if it hadn't made it to his consciousness or if he hadn't seen it voluntarily. I don't know, that could be, is what he says to me, but that he prefers to think it's something mystical, more his, more personal; that maybe that, this place, has a special energy or something, some significance. Yes, that could be, too. In fact it's already quite odd that the two of us are here in this moment, no? Don't you think? I guess so, he says, although I imagined it a thousand times. Are you for real? I ask him, as a figure of speech, and he says yes, and doesn't look at me. He's absorbed, he's looking ahead and chewing another sandwich. That's cool, I say, because I don't know what to say and then right away I realize it isn't clear whether I mean the fact that he imagined me in this place we're calling mystical or just the sandwich, so I try to clarify a little bit: I like this place, I say, it brings to mind all good things; the things, the images it evokes are good, as desolate as it is, this place.

31.

We've got water, plenty. We drink. The landscape
makes us thirsty. The idea that there's no water
here, that there isn't, that there might not be. It's
really hard for me to picture how I'll be supposed to
feel when I get back to Buenos Aires, when I'm there
again. Back in the desert, by the side of the truck,
I felt, in reality, so far from everything. Because we
were, because we are. From here, the city's major
streets like Callao and Corrientes seem somewhat
unreal, in fact impossible, a hallucination. I don't
want to go home, even if I don't know what my
home is, or maybe precisely because of this. Communicating in words, trying, attempting to communicate in words, by means of them. My stomach is a
little upset, probably from all the mate. And the car.
Being on the road this long makes me carsick, even
if it's in a truck. Even if I'm enjoying it. Even still,
it makes me carsick. Meaning there isn't even any
question of reading. I can't read in a car. I wouldn't
want to. I'd rather look out the window; there's
nothing in the world that could make me want to

miss what's happening out there. I hate not being able to read in motion. To read you have to be still, which is what I don't like about it. Or is reading in a vehicle reading in motion? I, for example, would love to be able to ride a bicycle and read or walk and read, but you can't. That's the whole thing: you read or you look, you can't do both. It's different if someone's reading to you. Traveling by car and having someone read to you . . . Although not that either, it's too much information, sooner or later I'd get distracted, I couldn't pay attention to what was being read to me, try to imagine it, and, at the same time, settle on the landscape or whatever it was that was out there, on the other side of the glass.

Today, after we ate, I fell asleep for quite a while, against the window. That, on the other hand, is something I can do without the slightest difficulty: fall asleep wherever. Like cats, like Ali. Some might say I'm a narcoleptic. Or that I'm depressed. It seemed a shame to me that that picnic had to end, but at a certain point the wind really picked up, and you couldn't be outside anymore, and besides, we had to keep going to make it to Trelew before nightfall, and so Juli could make his delivery. I feel a little scammed, I don't know why in my head the trip was going to be so much longer, probably because I made the same trip as a kid, and by bus, a pretty beat-up bus at that. I say we should keep going and spend the night in Madryn. Juli doesn't want to do that, he says that in Trelew there are more options, and they're cheaper, and that he doesn't have much interest in driving anymore, that he wants to have a real meal and a shower as soon as possible. That we can go to Madryn tomorrow, that he'll take me. We drive around the city for a little while until Juli comes across the exact address. I didn't remember that Trelew was like this. From the highway you access the city via a hill with dirt roads and little tiny houses, roads with puddles and stray dogs. Then, at some point, a few blocks in, the asphalt starts, and the city, the stores, little by little. Little businesses, very specific, very precise, staffed by their owners, or just about. We go around the square, there are quite a few people, quite a few people everywhere, in cars, on foot, on bikes, a lot of people. The plaza is pretty, *Independencia* I think I make out on a sign as we drive by, and then he turns right, we go two blocks further, and he stops in front of a shed/office. Juli gets out, I decide to wait for him in the car or next to the car. I put on your jacket and get out. It's really, really cold. The sun is very low, and there's nothing left now of its warmth. Nothing. I jump up and down a couple of times to warm myself up, to loosen up. I walk a little, exhale, release a white vapor. I clap, can't feel my hands, and a little dog comes up and snaps at me, from behind some bars, shrill, and it scares me. I walk down to the end of the block. The little houses are low, fairly similar to one another, except for the odd huge ranch-style here and there, super new and super ugly, those stand out. Or the ranch-style duplexes, there are also a few of those, brick facades, reflective glass, and tall bars painted black. Against what are they entrenching themselves, from what are they excluding themselves? It doesn't look like a particularly Patagonian set, with those bars, and those bricks, and those square houses that can do nothing to evade the wind. Why, in Patagonia, don't they build oval houses, or even round ones, invincible ones? No, ranch-style or tiny squares, in the Spanish style, circa eighteen ten, with railings and all, sheer nonsense; ranch-style houses with brick facades that—where do they even fire them? And why? With all the rock around. It is at the very least odd. I start back for the truck, the dog starts barking at me again, Julián isn't coming yet. I walk the other way, I can't stand still, and the cabin of the truck smells gross, like food, like breathing, like us. On the opposite corner, on a rectangle of grass, there's a small altar, a monolith of—once more—brick facade and concrete, painted white. It has two little glass doors and inside, a virgin. The typical image of the virgin, with a blue coat over a white dress, a tiara, hands together, smiling. The neighborhood altar is very tidy: a wreath of artificial flowers in colors faded by the sun, some candles, extinguished, and nothing more, no little medals or cards or coins or clothes, nothing. A tidy, cleared-off virgin. I spin around: a two-story house sits on the corner and on its wall graffiti saying *Guido genius*, *Condo Rock*, too, and a few more things, but in that skater-style writing I can't read. I wonder if the owner of the house with

these scrawlings is at the same time the altar's care-
taker. I find it funny, the coexistence of the little
virgin, so tidy, with the graffiti. I keep looking at
her awhile. It makes me feel something, generates
something: it's so strange the place she ended up in.
And nobody ever broke the glass that encases her,
even though it'd be so easy. There she is, so smug,
so erect, so healthy, placid; I look at this Mary, and I
like her now, I like the way she looks back, her tran-
quility, her blue hood, and her beauty on this little
corner, so far from everything, so near. I put my
hands together in an arch, look into her eyes and
lower my head, one, two, three times, like a Japanese
salutation while I think something, ask her for or
transmit something, I'm not sure what. I go back
towards the truck.

Does spring start tomorrow? I don't think so, not
quite yet.

32.

Let's go to Madryn, he says. He says he got us a good place to stay where they'll give us a discount, a family member of one of his friends. That he called and they'll be expecting us. I'm glad. And that it's just off the highway that runs along the coast, that's another nice thing, he says. That's fantastic, I say, I'm so glad, because I really am glad. I ask him if he doesn't mind driving more. No, no, he says, it's just another hour, and we'll be better off there, it's nicer. I'm glad, I'm happy, but I don't let it show too much. We go back towards the highway, I don't recognize the route. Trelew is very frenetic, there are a lot of people circulating, very fast, since it's the time of day when people get off work, they're all migrating, all going. Meanwhile something about the night ahead of us has activated me, excited me, not sexually, just excitement. Or perhaps sexually, too. I feel like having a very, very big cold beer in Madryn and getting dumb and tongue-tied, slowing myself down with alcohol and wanting everything very much, everything so much. And that appetite, from the cold, from the drive, is highly reminiscent of sexual appetite, so much so. The yearning is what is similar, so similar, too. I want to drink, I want to kiss, I want to dance, I want to see. I'll put on some music. Can I put on some music? I'd rather not, I want to listen to the night. I don't say that, I don't say the part about the night because he'd laugh at me, Julián would laugh. I roll down the window a little as we're driving towards the highway, so the cold will hit my face, and to smell the fragrance of Trelew. Right now the city doesn't smell that much, it just smells like cold, but once we're out where it's a little emptier it smells a little bit like grass, like trash, like dust, like night. I like night, like the ruckus. I like brushing up against a thing and not understanding it, feeling a fabric and being confused, a warmth in a fabric, a fragrance, an odor, something. And saliva and weight, the weight of the body, of someone else, against your clothing when it's cold, all that trapped there in a fabric, that thing of someone else's, that thing of someone else, that thing that makes everything so hypnotic. Seeing people in the darkness, seeing in the dark that so alters your perception, bundling up in darkness, against someone, against something, a back, a chest, something that envelops you/enfolds you, whispering, a little, between kisses and kisses, going back to someone's mouth like a stab, a new one, a renovated one, throwing yourself at the other, onto, getting it back, that mouth, a mouth, again, and starting everything over, everything over, tongue, the smell of the mouth and of its contours, of the contours of that mouth, not all salivas dry the same. No, not at all, an omen, a portent, losing track of the other person's components of where they are, of how they're distributed, which feature of the face is which, which part of the mouth is which, difference in sizes, distortion of sizes, of proportions and space, distortion of a cheek against another, near/far/in, how rough it is, what it isn't. Nocturnal places filled with smoke and bodies and possibilities, even though not always, but proximity and that dragging yourself, dragging yourself towards, against those other bodies, and at times, and at moments, going in, going into it, into that, into everything, going. Stealing a little bit of themselves when they're not looking, carefully, so they don't notice, or so they do, so they do notice and even so can't accuse you of anything, of anything you can't defend yourself against.

It's true the trip is not that long, and the route is unusual: all straight. I mean: it rises and falls, because of the landscape, which is hills, but the route itself is all straight. Then, from atop the hills you can see very, very far, see the long line of lights that leads into Madryn. As for the rest, you can't see any of the landscape, because there isn't much to see, and because there's no light left. The line that is the road seems suspended, a long corridor like a bridge over nothingness itself. You don't always get good things out of fantasies, nor do they always follow a useful path. We're silent but chewing mint gum to not fall asleep. Every so often, on this long road, Juli puts his hand on my knee, the hand he uses to shift gears, since he almost doesn't need it, he rests it on my left knee. I take it, put my hand over his, and I stroke it, just a little, just a tiny bit, just to acknowledge it, really, just that. It's gone now, that tension, from before, from talking, from having to say things, explain. And my stupid thing of wounded pride is mostly gone as well, and my wanting to pester him with questions about his family, and my wanting to be a mother and to know are gone. Now, here on this road, we are suspended in time, we're not in it, this line that we trace with the car is outside of the plan, the net, the structure. We're coming from and going to, but there isn't any here, this road does not exist, it's just us suspended, holding hands between the lights, on seats, with no music, no cigarettes, no coffee, no mate, no needs, with only night, nothing else.

33.

The place is called something like the Solar Inn or
Sun Inn. No, Solar. It's a new building, with two
stories and—yet again—a brick facade, but pol-
ished, unpainted. Our room doesn't have a view of
the sea, we're at the back of the building, which
looks out onto the garden of some neighbors, with
receptacles/ugly lawn decor and a wild dog. In our
room the decor and the furniture is neutral, not
very decisive, but fairly new and tidy, agreeable, everything pretty white. The first thing Julián does
when we get there is take a shower, and it's a long
shower. I don't know what's going to happen, now
I'm kind of nervous. The matter of the double bed
scares me a little, de-erotifies me, even if maybe it's
just an issue with the light, so white, and of the ex-
cessive euphoria in the car. Now I really could feel
like I've been married to Julián for ages, that we're
a married couple, that he's my husband and I'm his
old lady, and I'm keeping him company on a busi-
ness trip. In fact he asks me to get him his tooth-
brush from his bag. And I do. I know he brushes

his teeth in the shower, it's not a habit he would have given up. Fortunately he takes it from me by sticking his arm out, I wouldn't have known what to do with his naked body. I tell him I'm going to get some beer, he asks where, I say around here, he says around here there isn't anything, I'd have to walk a ton, and it's way too cold. That I should just wait a second, for him, and that we'll drive into the city center. I'd rather walk, I say, we already spent the entire day in the truck. All the more reason to wait for him, he says, that we'll go out to eat in the city center, and we'll walk.

Juli comes out of the bathroom in his boxers, I don't look directly at him, but I can tell. I keep writing. Aren't you going to shower, you animal? Not now, I'll do it when we get back. If I shower now I'll be too cold. I feel like a steak. I feel like beer. Let's go.

It's fucking freezing outside, a different kind of cold than in Esquel, this one's an ocean cold. We cross the highway and go to the beach, to see the water. But you can't see the ocean that well because it's nighttime, and it's just a huge black form, immobile and sounding, noisy and dark. And on the shore it's really cold, because of the wind, a very strong one. Julián cries out into the night, at the ocean, and he grabs me from behind, and he hugs me, wrings me out as best he can with all that jacket in between us. Fortunately I don't quite manage to feel him completely, all that fabric prevents me, but he hugs me this way and I lean my head back and lean into him, on his shoulder and look out at the water and am a little less cold, and I like it, of course I like him holding me and hugging me this way, but I'm not sure if I feel like having this turn into a little romantic escapade, an ocean love story, couple on the beach, reunion, I don't know what I want. I hate that he can have everything: wife, kids, family, lover, it's all so easy for him, all so great, ready to go. I hate it, I hate that I'm attracted to him and that he can have me, and on the other hand everything is so finite, such finitude, that I do feel a little bit like going all the way with the whole rose-colored picture and kiss him on the beach and have those ballads playing and say certain things to each other and then leave tomorrow. But, now, that sappiness destroys me almost as much as the double bed, there's something so predictable about it that really wrecks me. I think I would have preferred the crash in the desert; it suits me better. I say I'm hungry and I'm cold and I want to go. Aren't you going to give me a kiss? he says, and I say no, and he says screw you.

We walk pretty fast, to warm up, the neutrality of the fabric of my jeans doesn't help much, it does nothing against the cold. But the friction of my knees in movement helps quite a bit to warm up the denim, and in this way it works. We barely talk, white vapor comes out in clouds from our mouths. Madryn isn't bad, not bad at all. I remembered it as being quite a bit uglier, industrial, and with no trees, but no, it turns out to be nice. It's quite a few blocks till we get to the center itself; it takes a while before we start to see all the stores that sell reproductions of whales and penguins in wool and metal and ceramic and stuffed and T-shirt and mate and photographic and rubber versions. We go by a couple of bars for young people—some of them with pool tables, others with draft beer, or big bottles of beer—but we're not fully convinced. We want to eat. Juli says he knows a grill where you can get just about anything, Don Román or San Román, something with Román. It's on the north side of the city. Almost a cantina. Behind the door where you go in there's a foul smell lurking, a powerful whiff of food and frying, very powerful. The grill and the guy manning it—believe it or not—are inside. We're on the verge of changing our minds, but the cold at our heels and the prospect of walking more around Madryn in denim dissuades us, and we enter into that intangible material odor. The vibe is that of an old tavern subjected to renovations less cheap than in poor taste. There's an annexed room that is remarkably different, with a white lacquered floor, glistening, and the walls are tile, too, with paper in various shades of pink, and matching tablecloths. The chairs have a plastic covering over another pink, yet another shade. They seat us in that room, the newer room, and the easier one to clean, the one they probably feel proud of. We look at each other again: it's now or never, if we want to flee, but we don't do it. I'd be too embarrassed at this point already. I choose to believe that for whatever reason I deserve or we deserve this odor, these shades of fake pastel. On the walls there are maps—some comic, others not—of Madryn, the Valdés Peninsula, photos of their most valued fauna—orca, whale, whale calf, sea lion, seal—and other adornments more themed around the puna: tapestries and Inca-ish things, or what looks like that, photos or paintings of llamas or guanacos, more Andean. And to top it all off every now and then a Coca-Cola decoration/ souvenir, those things they have at pseudo-country-club-type places, family country clubs. My back is to the room, I see the wall, Juli, the restaurant. On the table, some paper place mats with, once more, animals. They're photocopied photos, in colors. Each one has a different animal on it with a little caption giving some information about that species. Juli gets a fox, I get a whale. My whale is in blues and his fox in oranges. We look at them, discuss them. I hate that I got the whale, it depresses me, Juli laughs. I hate having to know that it's a cetacean mammal, and that it comes up to the coasts around here once a year to reproduce. The waiter comes over to our table and tells us that if we like them we can take them with us, that's what they're for. How awful, the worst is that later, because the waiter and his offer make me sad, I'll end up taking the place mat with the gigantic cetacean folded up into fourths in my jacket so that the waiter doesn't feel bad or think we were making fun of his place mats. I order a beer, blessed beer, and Juli gets wine. To stomach the stench, which, psychological or not, has already attached itself to my palate. There isn't any beer smaller than three quarters of a liter, so I start off with that, and then I'll get in on the wine. Juli orders a steak with french fries, I add a salad and another steak. The beer does me a lot of good, the bread does the beer a lot of good. The basket comes with those little old-fashioned Provençal toasts: they smell like the tavern, I'm not up to it, I prefer the sponginess of the little black rolls. They bring *leber*, two slices. Juli eats it, I prefer butter with salt.

"You happy, babe?"

"You know, I actually am, you know, I actually really am quite happy. I hate to admit it, but I am."

"Me too, I'm happy too. I'm happy to see you, I'm happy you're here; I'm happy we're here."

"Just me and you and a portion of *leber*."

"What?"

"Nothing," I laugh. "It's from *Reality Bites*. About making do with not very much, just that."

"You look really pretty, you know?"

"I am really pretty."

"Yes, you are, but that's not what I mean. I remembered you were pretty, but now you look pretty in a different way."

"Different how?"

"Older."

"More worn?"

"Maybe."

"It's the city."

"Maybe, in any case it suits you."

"Well, thanks. You look hot."

"Fuck off."

"I mean it, the beard works for you; fatherhood too. Even if fatherhood looks better on you with the kids off in the distance."

"You're such a piece of shit."

"The point is you look hot."

"You're not going to kiss me at any point tonight, idiot?"

"I don't know."

"I just want to know so I can get ready."

"You look red."

"You too, it's the wine."

"It's this dump. Doesn't it stink?"

"It definitely does. I think I'm used to it now, but when we came in it really stank."

The waiter is a little bit intimidating; he and his colleague, in reality. They're circling around the room where we are the whole time, and it's not that busy, with their backs to the walls and watching everything. I guess it's part of their job, being attentive and at the ready, but it really does get a little bit intimidating, because they see everything we do at every moment. I feel like they can even hear. Every so often waiter number two, the younger one, takes his phone out of his apron and sends or receives messages. Or is he checking the time? In any case, they have very prominent roles this evening. The salad comes out, and it's really good, plentiful and fresh, and shortly thereafter the steaks and the fries come out too. The least appetizing thing is the fries, in the end, who would have thought, with that oil smell overpowering everything. But between the steaks and the salad and the wine it works out totally fine. Not to mention the company, of course, that goes without saying. I feel the alcohol settling, feel it working. I switched from beer to wine a while ago already, and perhaps, only perhaps, it was too fast. Now I can feel it in my face, I imagine it's the food, too, and I tell myself to stop chugging it, even if it's just a little break I take. My mouth feels kind of numb, relaxed, and I know perfectly well that it will—inevitably—turn into/end in wanting to make out. The steak makes my stomach happy, and everything seems to be getting good. I feel, I've been feeling, for a while up to now, very good. Who could take that away from me? Juli is attractive, he eats and is attractive. It's appealing watching him eat, looking at him. He's starving and very focused on his prey. Every so often he lets a *this is good* escape, onto his plate, onto his steak, which doesn't expect a response, doesn't have any expectations, which is just singing to his meal, singing its praises. He becomes childlike when he eats, which makes him touching. His brown hair falls almost to his shoulders, lightly curly and messy, from the wind, from the walk. He has thick eyebrows, kind of reddish, and his beard, too, his beard is also different colors, a little copper, a little bit brighter red, slightly golden, too, every so often. Very uneven, I hadn't seen him with a beard in forever. In fact I don't think I ever saw him with a beard, it's more of a fatherly thing. He's more angular, the life of a grown-up, I suppose, responsibility, that kind of sinks his eyes, the cavities of his eyes, and makes the circles underneath them more pronounced. And those dark circles call, in turn, more attention to his brown eyes, makes you see them more. Although they are sort of set back, that sitting back and the darkness of his skin brings them out somehow, makes you see them. Fuck, he has nice eyes. Beautiful eyes. All these changes, a domino effect of changes set off by that beard, the presence of so much hair on his face. Or adulthood, that could also be it. The sweater he's wearing is very sweet: a wool cardigan, big, made of wool in different shades of brown, mottled, with a brown zipper, too. It has a broad collar, the cardigan, and it looks really good on him, with his face, his hair, his jeans. Lord almighty, the wine in my head is beginning to wreak havoc.

"That sweater is so *ñoño*," I tell him, as he chews. I finished eating a while ago and am now nourishing myself with alcohol, a base of barley and grape, and I gave up, very politely, a portion of my generous steak. "Did your mom knit it for you?"

"Yes indeed," he says, still chewing. "What is that, that's a new word, is it like popular at school or something?"

"What, *ñoño*?"

"Uh-huh."

"No, idiot, I think it's from *The Simpsons*, from the

Mexican dubbing. I always said *ñoño*. Me and my brother always said it."

"I don't remember."

"Well, I guess you remember what you want to."

"Look who's talking."

"All right, enough with the belligerence, it's exhausting. Your cardigan looks great on you."

"Thank you."

"It's very sweet."

"You're drunk."

"I might be. Are you not?"

"A little bit, maybe."

He finishes the steak, pounds down the last little battered potato, wipes the fat off his hands, his mouth, with a napkin, and takes my hand. He reaches out over the table, over the side with the fauna place mats and takes my hand. He pushes the sleeve of my sweater a little bit back, with the tips of his fingers, and he takes the whole of my hand, all of it, touching it all. Immediately—this is what it is—I get turned on. I mean: it hurts, my cunt hurts, awakens, I don't know how to talk about this, but something gets switched on, desire, maybe. And it's just a hand, even just that. I guess I would kiss him now, but he pours me some more wine, with the hand that isn't touching me, he orders another bottle with a gesture that is almost unnecessary because the waiters are practically in our faces, and he asks me if I want dessert, asks, Would you like dessert? And I mean I don't know, like, sure. When the wine comes they bring the menu back, and we want ice cream with chocolate and dulce de leche, with two spoons, to share. I'm doing it for him, I want very little of it, of the ice cream, just to soften slightly the harshness of the red wine on my tongue, to balance out that bitterness. And I keep drinking the wine, imbibing. We're not going to finish this other bottle. Julián asks if we can take it with us, the waiter grants us this and brings us a cork, a different one, not from this bottle. Taking the wine to go reminds me of the place mat, so I fold up the whale and put it in my pocket. It has a few vinegar or lettuce stains, but whatever. We pay the check, we bundle up, we go out. Behind us that odor, before us, the cold. We go left, towards the coast, we're half a block away. At the corner we come across a bale of hay, the kind you always see in Westerns—like the tumbleweeds that roll through the desert, symbols of *there's nothing going on here*—but the weird thing about this one is that it's in a city. A coastal city. It makes us laugh because basically we're very drunk, because it's bizarre that it's here and because it is— it really is—very big. I suggest we take it, we drag it a few feet, people are looking at us, I sort of trip, and we let it go. We pass by a cool bar, and Juli suggests we go in to have a nightcap, a couple of whiskeys. I remind him of the bottle of wine, suggest we go drink it somewhere. He suggests we go back to the hotel. I say no, that I want to go somewhere natural, in nature, to the beach, for example. Juli says that there's no way he's going to the beach in this cold, that it's just that right now I'm drunk and I don't really realize, but that tomorrow I'm going to want to die on the bus dribbling snot all over. So then what, I say. He suggests getting the truck and heading for the peninsula. Now? I say. What's wrong with now? he says. Now is great because there's no one on the road, and we can go to this spot on Punta Flecha that has an amazing view, it's like ten miles away, maybe we'll be able to see a whale or something still. I don't want to, I say, I hate whales, they scare me, their heads are covered in crustaceans. Don't be an idiot, he says, at this time of night you can't see anything anyway, in terms of animals, but the view from there is really pretty, there's this wooden path and the whole trajectory is great. Are you going to drive like this, drunk? I say. We'll go slow, and there's nobody out now anyway. Okay, fine, I say. We walk back to get the truck, walking quickly, singing, "Palm Tree." *Days go by, minds change. / What was a meadow, is now a lion / or it's a cat with dreads and leprosy / and it isn't my imagination.*

"What did you say?"

"What?"

"Did you say, Or it's a cat with dreads?" I ask.

"Yeah."

"That's not how it goes! It's, Or it's a cat with harsh and leprosy."

"You're insane, what the fuck would that even mean?"

"What would a cat with dreads mean? You're totally out of it."

"You're the one who's totally out of it, what the fuck would a cat with harsh be?"

"I don't know, I always sang it that way, I never saw the lyrics . . . Are you sure it says *dreads?*"

"I mean, I think so, now you're making me question, but I think so, it's more logical."

"I guess so."

I tell him I'm cold, he tells me he'll run up ahead and get the truck and come back for me, that I can keep walking in the meantime, and that we'll meet in the middle. He runs off, I wonder if he'll actually come back, if he'll remember that he left me back here, or if he'll just go back to the hotel and pass out. I sing to myself, to warm myself up as I walk: *The tree measures time in its trunk. / I look alienated around. / I'm in the middle of a palm tree / between green leaves I think I am . . .* Or was it of you, *between green leaves I think of you?* And then the thing is that I think of you, suddenly, like a kick in the ass, you come back to me, you. It's the nineties, and it's you. Teenagers in the nineties, the twenty-first century now finds us ridiculous, already discards us. So the nineties with a little of the eighties, that comeback, maybe, is what makes us who we are. And twenty-whatever or two thousand, I never really knew what you were supposed to say, I guess two thousand, in any case two-thousand you is essentially nothing, you barely got in there. Fuck, now here, in this euphoria, with Juli, with the south, with the cold, with the alcohol, with the decade, the last decade, the one that made us, I think of you. You come to me, you appear to me in the night, the fact that you're not here appears to me, that I can't tell you this even though I pretend like I can, not being able to ever tell you is still something I can't understand. That you could have taken so long to decompose, too, that, too, I can't believe there's still so much left of you, down there, buried, hair and things like that, skin. I don't want to take anything, I never wanted to, and I would give (I don't know what, not everything because then you wouldn't be there, but I'd give a lot) so much to be able to tell you, for real, to see you, to sing a song with you, shout it out hugging each other, have you over to my apartment, for you to get to know my house and my boyfriend, the one I have now, and have him get to know you and have you tell me which one's better, which one you like better, if it's Juli, if it's him, even though obviously you would like Manuel better, and in reality you wouldn't care about either of them, because the two of us is enough, there's nothing else, we never needed anything else, although we did.

You can't imagine how much I'd give to dance with you, leaping around, just one more time, hugging each other or not, in a crowd, see you move away, come back in the middle of a mosh, so far away, so close, get back closer by elbowing everyone, crash into everyone, bursting out laughing, see your gestures, your distorted laughter, close, far, coming, going, set up among all those people, and me, too, and we shouted and shouted amidst those people, all the lyrics, songs. Or we swore to one another declarations of eternal love, undying friendship, the purest form of love over tables at bars, wood carvings on tables with other kinds of inscriptions, from other romances, other declarations, eternal promises, unconditional eternal promises over wooden tables at dirty bars with peanut shells and rotten peanuts and the halo of beer losing its chill and having that excess, that overflow of beer go onto the sleeve of your sweater, of your jacket, maybe even of this jacket that I'm wearing now. And hugging you over that table, with beer and peanuts and little pet names and inscriptions, hugging each other and swearing things for all time and having people look at us, and us just promising each other all those things, forever.

34.

He honks. I must look sad. I'm sitting on the curb
with my head between my legs, my hair hanging
off of my head, your hood on, all crying. What are
you doing, dummy, get in. I get in. What are you
doing crying? he asks. I just remembered you, I
say. That I miss you. Well, yeah, stupid, he says. I
say, but no, that it's been ages since I felt this way.
That "Palm Tree" killed me, I say, that the nineties
kill me. He brushes back the hair off my face and in
the same movement he kisses me, comes completely over me. I don't get what's happening, of course
I reciprocate the kiss, I mean, I don't reciprocate it
so much as just be very there to receive it, so there.
It's really warm, his mouth is really warm on the
inside. That's good, and it's soft. I can't help but
get a little dizzy when I close my eyes, it's that I'm
drunk, and that I miss you. We kiss very deeply,
you know what that's like, when you kiss when you
love each other. That's what I mean, those kisses
that are everything, the ones where you can barely tell yourself apart from the other person, the

ones where you get inside the other person, where you put the other person inside yourself, and your tongues come and go, getting so big and so alive while your eyes are shut, like wet vermin, slippery, searching. After a long while the kiss ends, we hold each other, I bury myself in his sheepskin, in the little bits of wool, and I wipe off the spit he left on me, we left on me. He holds me, tight, and I cry. And I know I won't be able to stop crying at this point, something broke/let loose. All the times I didn't cry in Esquel come up now, want to come out, turn into tears. Now I can't stop crying, Juli asks me if I want to talk about it, I say no, I keep crying, and every once in a while I dive into his mouth. I cry and I kiss him, it's the only thing I can do right now. I don't want to talk, there's nothing to say, it's just a question of letting go. So kissing, crying, and hugging, hugging as rest, generating fluid, a lot of it. Crying and saliva. From all this crying the dizziness of drunkenness gradually starts to transform into tiredness, exhaustion: as I regain my calm, I begin to fall asleep. Something about the heating in the car, too, a kind of stupor. As I'm falling asleep I'm still able to perceive that Juli is talking to me, whispering sweet things, loving things, petting my face, I will always love you, baby, always, and I want to reciprocate, respond, answer, but I can't, I'm numbed, by sadness, by kissing, just about gone. I know, because my body knows, that Juli has started the truck. I don't know where we're going, I let myself be taken, I'm gone.

"Besides I have my period."

"Blood doesn't bother me, I've witnessed child-birth. And it wouldn't be the first or the last time."

"I can't, you smell like baby, I don't know, like baby vomit."

"What are you talking about, dummy, my clothes are clean."

"It's not a smell that comes out in the wash, you've got the kid in your little sheepskin there."

"That's not from the kid, it's that shitty smell that stuck from the grill, you smell like that too. I'm in love with you."

"Stop, Juli."

"I mean it, I've always been in love with you."

"How would you know."

"How would you know, idiot, you're always running away."

"I'm always running away?"

"Yes."

"Besides, what good does it do me now that you're

in love with me? What do you expect to get out of it?"

"I don't want to get anything, I'm just telling you how it is."

"How it is is you've got a wife and two kids."

"What does that have to do with anything, sometimes it really surprises me how stupid you can be. What is this shit about cheap morality? You act like this sophisticated city girl who lives in Buenos Aires and yet, actually, you're an idiot."

"You're calling me an idiot, moron? I'm just trying to respect you and your family."

"What are you talking about, respect, you don't even know them, they're nothing to you."

"They are something, plus I'm doing it for myself, too, to protect myself a little."

"What are you doing here, then?"

"I don't know, I wanted to talk with you, because I missed you, because in the end in Esquel we didn't have a chance to talk at all."

"Are you attracted to me?"

"Why would you ask me that? I don't like the acid baby smell you've got on you."

"Come on, I'm not kidding."

"Well, don't ask me that, you know I am, I told you yesterday already, you're beautiful."

"So?"

"I don't know, I can't."

"I'm going to kill you."

"Fine, hit me."

"Don't provoke me, you know that if you tell me to hit you it makes me want to fuck you."

"You turn me on so much."

"So stop screwing around, then, I've wanted to fuck you since I saw you."

"At the bar?"

"I don't know, was that where it was?"

"Yeah, we saw each other at Vanina's bar for the first time . . . This time, I mean."

"Yeah, I guess so."

"Well, why didn't you say anything? You just took me home like it was no big deal."

"When?"

"That night, after the bar, you dropped me at Andrea's place like it was nothing, you didn't even kiss me."

"I don't understand what you're talking about, do you want to have sex or not?"

"You told me you were in love with me."

"Yes."

"Well, I don't think so, I don't think I want to have sex with you, in a little while I have to take a bus to Buenos Aires, go back to my boyfriend, forget about you, I don't know if I feel like it, it was so hard last time."

"So you'd rather nothing happen then? You'd rather just go on home like this?"

"Like what?"

"Turned on."

"Wouldn't be the first time."

"Come on, Emi, it isn't like that, you're mixing

everything up in my mind, we won't have sex if you
don't want to, it's not about sex, my life doesn't de-
pend on having sex with you. I don't feel like arguing anymore, if we keep arguing I'm going to get
even more turned on, I feel like you're talking in circles, I don't know, just come here, let me hold you."

He holds me. The one who's turned on now is me.
I can't take it anymore. Even though it's not exactly being turned on, because I'm not, in general: I
wouldn't feel like touching myself or like being with
anybody else. It's him, it's my hangover, it's this moment, and it's him. And it's us. I rest my head on
his shoulder, put my head in his neck, breathe there.
He smells so good, as true as the acidity thing is, it
doesn't bother me, it coexists well with that smell
that's so familiar to me, his smell, his sweat, his person smell. I try not to exhale right on his neck because I'm confused, and I don't want to keep driving
him crazy. It would appear to all be vastly simpler
for him. He thinks he's in love with me but that he's
already given me up, meaning he can be in love with
me in this passive way, think of me from that place,
in parts, in fragments of me, of what I am or of
what he wants me to be, he selects me, selects my
portions, keeps me, preserves me in his memory in a
very particular way, resurrecting me when he wants
to, and it's melancholy, a memory of that which
could have been, and this would be the saddest fuck
in the world, and the most beautiful all at once. Today we'll say goodbye to each other, and he'll think

of me for three more days, as he goes back in his truck and every time he passes by the little picnic tree and everything will be so sad and so lovely and so definitive, and then he'll get home where his son and his wife's pregnancy and his new son are awaiting him, not to mention when that one is born, and by then everything will have become so relative, and I will gradually fade away, the memory of me will grow opaque, a few images in sepia, difficult to appreciate, so relative all in all, so relative. But not me, I, on the other hand, will cry the whole way back, and that is just the beginning of the end because at least I'm still in transit, the worst part comes later, when I have to get my life back, grab the bull by the horns, put my place back together, my relationship with Manuel, tell him I cheated on him with Julián or not that I cheated because it's not like it was about or against Manuel, but that I was with Julián, and then have Manuel get bitter and rightfully so and have him feel bad thinking that part of my sadness over the next few days or weeks is going to be due to Julián, to that presence that isn't that and that I brought on me, and me rocking, juggling, thinking that everything I have around me reeks and that I'm never going to completely know exactly what I want and that maybe I'm always wrong and then neither leaving nor staying, nor anything, neither being anywhere, nor being anywhere.

36.

Dead girlfriends, that's the theme of it, dead young girlfriends. Dead girls who, meanwhile, at times seem to return from the dead. At times. Vincent Gallo covers a vast expanse, on the highway, listening to music and meeting girls. They all have names of flowers: Violet, Lily, Rose. But he's looking for Daisy. En route he stops at Daisy's childhood home. Her mother is there, and a grandmother in a vegetable state. And a brown rabbit that apparently belongs to this Daisy. The mother assures him it's the same rabbit from before. Vincent asks her about Daisy, the mother says it's been ages since she's heard from her, and she asks the same things over and over again. Here we learn that Daisy and Vincent have known each other since they were kids. Vincent starts back on his journey, stops his truck at some salt flats and gets out to keep going on a motorcycle. He finally makes it to California. He goes to this house to look for Daisy, but she won't open the door. He leaves her a note. He goes to a hotel to wait for her. And she comes, in the end she comes, and it's

Chloë Sevigny dressed up like a secretary, wearing a little suit. The encounter is highly disturbing, she goes to take drugs in the bathroom, he asks her to stop, tells her he loves her, she tells him she loves him, she wants to sit on his lap, he kind of doesn't want her to but does, and you don't really understand why, why all this suffering if they love each other so much, but you get that something terrible must have happened in the past, but you don't know what, you just don't know. The point is that indeed at some point Chloë sits down on his lap, then I think they make out, he takes off her blouse and I'm pretty sure her bra too, I can't quite remember, and then she starts sucking his dick, just like that, for real, porn in the foreground, and Vincent Gallo's dick is clearly going very well for them, it's huge, you can see the veins, and she takes it all in her mouth, and he's saying to her, like, as he brushes her hair from her face, he's saying in this way with all this pathos in it, swear to me you'll never suck another guy's cock, swear to me you'll never suck another guy's cock, and she, with his dick down her throat, makes a few guttural sounds as though giving him to understand that yes, I mean, that no, that she will not suck any other guy's cock, ever, and it's all very sad and very awful. In the end he comes and lies down on the bed, desperately sad, and she lies down beside him and tries to console him, but he cannot be consoled, and they start talking about something, about a night when something happened, something terrible, something irrevocable, and then you finally get the flashback and find out.

So apparently one night in the past they went to this concert together, and she was a little bit high and drunk and went to the bathroom by herself, and she was followed by some guys who gave her something or other to smoke, which she thought was marijuana, but actually she ended up unconscious, and they raped her, the three or four of them all raped her, and the tragic thing is that he, Vincent, at some point realizes that she hasn't come back and it's been forever and he goes to look for her, and he sees her, he sees her being fucked, but he doesn't realize she's passed out, and he leaves! He leaves! Here we have the tragic error, he leaves because he is mistaken, because he reads the situation wrong, and he comes back hours later, and at that point there's an ambulance there that's taken her, taking Daisy away, and she—back in present day—is telling him how she was left there lying on the floor and that she threw up and that since she was unconscious she choked to death on her own vomit. And she asks him, Why did you leave, why didn't you help me? And he says, What happened? What happened? And she says, Well, I died. And at first you don't understand, and then you do; she tells him a few times that she died, and you see her on the stretcher with her face covered up by the white sheet, and you're wondering if maybe they managed to revive her. But no, she just died, she actually died, and then you go back to the present in the hotel and realize he was alone in the bed and that Daisy isn't there anymore and that she never was, like the brown rabbit.

37.

I don't feel like having breakfast at this point. The orange juice doesn't sound appealing, the yogurt even less so, the little croissants. I have a piece of dry toast, to see if it will maybe help with my hangover. I look out the window. Juli, to my left, eats a little bit of everything. He doesn't say anything. I breathe in the steam from my tea. I look ahead, at the ocean, the sun. My head is killing me, the circles under my eyes are gigantic, and I'm carsick. I think about the long trip that awaits me, and on the one hand I feel like being alone, like being alone again, and on the other hand I'm afraid of being carsick, throwing up, feeling lousy, not seeing him again. He finishes his breakfast, looks at me, touches my hand. I look at him, I smile, weakly. He asks me if I feel any better, I tell him no, he says, screw you.

We fill up the gas, get onto the coastal highway, it's a beautiful day. I look out the window, I'm on the ocean side. I roll it down a little, being closed in makes me sicker. I realize I don't remember anything from last night, that after falling asleep, nothing. I hate that, it makes me nauseous. We get to the bus station, very fast, it was so close by car. Juli asks me if I want him to come with me, to get my ticket, to wait, I tell him no, that I'd rather he didn't. He takes my bag out, puts it on the sidewalk, looks at me. I feel like shit, typical distracting symptom: instead of being able to think about this goodbye, my stomach starts to cramp up, I feel like I need to get to a bathroom as soon as possible, and in this way I make everything as short and sweet as possible. He takes my hands, he looks at me, but I'm inwards, I don't look at him that much, I don't want to connect, he asks me to take care, he says he loved seeing me, I nod, I don't say anything, he hugs me, I stay stiff, tense in his arms, I barely pat his shoulder, he perceives it and backs away, looks at me and says, you're such a shit. Never more apt.

He lets go of my hands, gets into the truck, and starts it. Vapor is released from the exhaust pipe, the truck rumbles and from behind my hair I can only see the bumper, and now that bumper is moving off into the distance, exiting my field. And that's it. I pick up my bag and hustle inside the station to look for a bathroom.

I hear water running. There's music playing far away, although it's loud. Ceasing to function as I'm used to doing. Not going to bus stations, going with. Not saying goodbye. Is that still water, or are people applauding? There are tiny sheets of things coming loose from my teeth, I don't know what they are, they could be bits of bread or could be my teeth eroding; since they already were before, and now they're just dissolving, dissolving, and now my neck starts hurting. Begins. And later not being asked a thing, anything more. Ridiculousness. Not being anywhere. Not being here or here or here or here, and doing it all the same. Like inviting someone out for dinner, someone very special, and having them not come. And having them not ask you anything: not what you've been up to, not what you're planning on doing, not to mention how you plan to do it. Just nothing at all. You don't know what all this means, do you? Do you know what it means? Kissing is nothing and everything. Having things within reach and not knowing how to ask for them, how to get to them. An image of yourself that's out of focus. A blurring of oneself, of one's form, an outline. Resembling only scantly your own ideal, resembling yourself so little at times. Not wanting to let go nor being able to hold on, having it slip through your hands, through your fingers, like you, like your things, like your remnants, parts of something, of a friend, too, fragments of a friend who's not there, who doesn't exist. Being supposed to want to converge with the closest thing to the best version of yourself, and turning around, turning around and around the thing that isn't there, as though magnetized, as though stupefied, as though magnetically drawn and repelled at the same time, like that. Finding yourself face-to-face again against a thing you can neither detect nor avoid. Me here and on the other side you. I carry that, enormous, in my arms, and I don't see what, and I stay holding what isn't in this way, stuck to a nucleus of something that defines a here and another here, that can neither be seen nor touched, that's all.

It's only later, on a bench in the sun, on the embankment, with a mangy dog at my feet, a friendly dog, a transition dog, that I can wreck myself a little when I reach inside my pocket and come across the smelly place mat, the whale place mat in my right pocket. The whale, the dog with mange, all broken. My mangy dog licks the place mat, rips it up, eats it in shreds, blue, of whale, of fat, of animal, seeking the stain; the whale, in the dog's mouth.

The Feminist Press is a nonprofit educational organization founded to amplify feminist voices. FP publishes classic and new writing from around the world, creates cutting-edge programs, and elevates silenced and marginalized voices in order to support personal transformation and social justice for all people.

See our complete list of books at
feministpress.org